1 of 8

John Glenn

Young Astronaut

illustrated by Robert S. Brown

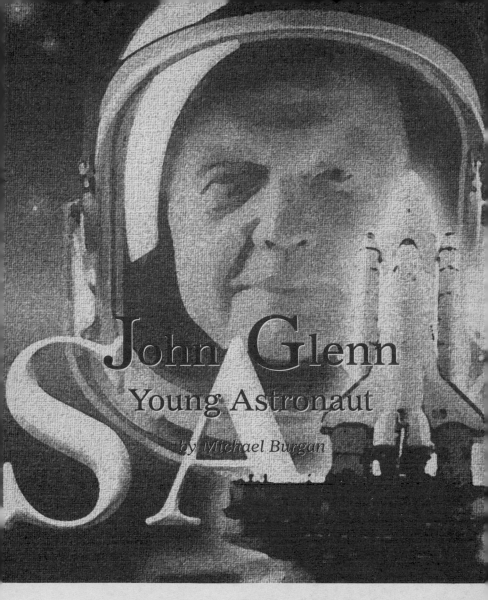

John Glenn
Young Astronaut

by Michael Burgan

ALADDIN PAPERBACKS

New York London Toronto Sydney Singapore

T 7000

First Aladdin Paperbacks edition September 2000

Aladdin Paperbacks
An imprint of Simon & Schuster Children's Publishing Division
1230 Avenue of the Americas
New York, NY 10020

The text for this book was set in Adobe Garamond
Printed and bound in the United States of America.
2 4 6 8 10 9 7 5 3 1

Library of Congress Catalog Card Number: 00-106363

ISBN: 0-689-83397-0

Illustrations

Contents

John Glenn

Young Astronaut

First Flight

"Listen to those tires hum, Bud."

"I hear it, Dad."

"And feel the wind in your face."

Eight-year-old John Glenn, Jr., nodded as the warm breeze brushed his cheeks. What a day! The summer sun was shining, red and blue wildflowers dotted the roadside, and his father was taking him on a car trip. They were only going to nearby Cambridge, not far from the Glenns' home in New Concord, Ohio. But to John, it was still a great adventure. He liked riding along the road, moving, feeling the speed of the car on the brick highway.

Mr. Glenn was on his way to a job. John Herschel Glenn, Sr., was a plumber in New Concord. He sometimes had work in Cambridge. John, Jr.—Bud, to his family—had been born in Cambridge in 1921. But John didn't remember much about his years there. The Glenn family had moved to New Concord when he was still a toddler.

It only took Mr. Glenn a few minutes to check out the plumbing job in Cambridge. Then the father and son were back on the road.

"Bud," Mr. Glenn said. "Look over there."

John followed his father's finger as it pointed over to the left. "A plane!" John cried.

"Want to take a closer look?" Mr. Glenn asked.

"Could we, Dad? Please?"

Mr. Glenn slowed the car and turned off the road. The small plane sat in a field. Airports in the 1920s were simple. Sometimes they were only a strip of mown grass in a meadow. Mr. Glenn stopped the car near the plane, and John scrambled out.

A man stood near the plane, tinkering with its engine. He wore a leather jacket, and a pair of goggles sat high on his head. He must be the pilot. John thought he looked like Steve Canyon, a hero from the comic strips. The man looked up as John ran over. "Hey there, sport," the pilot said.

"Hello, sir," John replied.

The man smiled as Mr. Glenn approached the plane. "Polite kid you got here, mister."

"We try," Mr. Glenn said. He walked beside the plane. "She's a beauty. Don't you think so, Bud?"

John could only nod silently. He was in awe. He stared at the wings and imagined what it would be like to fly. Driving in the car was okay, but to be up in the air! Soaring over the trees, over the houses in New Concord, flying across the country!

"Don't get too close, Bud," Mr. Glenn warned. "You don't want to break anything."

"He can't hurt it," the pilot said. "Go ahead, sport, touch the wing."

"Dad?" John asked, looking at his father. Mr. Glenn smiled.

"You know what this is?" the pilot asked.

"A biplane," John replied. "But I'm not sure what kind."

"She's a Waco. And she flies really sweet."

"I bet," John said. He noticed two open cockpits in the small plane. John imagined himself in front, flying the Waco. Straight up, and then down fast, and into a loop, then turning, turning—

"Bud?" Mr. Glenn's voice snapped John out of his daydream. "Did you hear me?"

"N-no, sir," John said hesitantly.

Mr. Glenn crouched down next to his son. "I said, if you like, we can go up."

"In the plane?"

"Well, I don't think we can get the car more than a few feet off the ground. Come on, I bet we can work out something with the pilot here." The two men smiled and winked at each other.

"You mean it?" John asked his father.

14

"Of course I do. And if you don't want to go up, I'll just have to go by myself."

John began to bounce up and down. "No, no, Dad, I want to, I want to!"

Mr. Glenn looked at the pilot. "You think he really wants to?" He took out his wallet, handed the pilot a few bills, then climbed into the rear cockpit.

The pilot boosted John into the seat after him. "All strapped in?" the pilot asked.

"All set," Mr. Glenn said.

"Then let's fly!"

The pilot climbed in and started the engine. The Waco's roar filled John's ears as the plane rolled down the grassy strip. He could barely see out of the cockpit. But John could *feel* the motion, the increasing speed. Suddenly he lurched back in his seat. They were off the ground! Mr. Glenn tried to talk over the buzz of the engine, but all John heard was the air rushing all around him. The plane banked to the left, and John could finally see the earth below them. The houses and barns in Cambridge looked like the little toy buildings he made out of blocks. John wanted the flight to go on forever, but in a few minutes they were back at the airfield. The plane bounced along the grass before coming to a stop.

"What did you think?" the pilot asked.

John sat back for a moment in his seat. "It was . . . I mean . . . wow!"

"I think he liked it," Mr. Glenn said.

John still fumbled for words. "I felt like . . . it was . . . I felt like I was Charles Lindbergh!"

The two men laughed.

"So you know all about 'Lucky Lindy,' do you?" the pilot asked.

"Sure I do," John answered. "Everybody does."

Two years before, Charles Lindbergh made aviation history. On a long, lonely, dangerous flight, Lucky Lindy flew from New York to France without stopping. It was the first solo flight across the Atlantic Ocean. When Lindbergh returned to the United States, he was a hero.

"Dad read all the newspaper stories to me,"

John continued. "And I've seen pictures of his plane."

"Ah, the *Spirit of St. Louis,*" the pilot said.

John nodded. "And one day we saw him flying over us, when he was going to Columbus."

"Now, Bud, we don't know—"

"But, Dad, you said Mr. Lindbergh was flying to Columbus."

"Yes, but—"

"And you said he had to fly over New Concord on his way there."

"I know, but—"

"So maybe that *was* Mr. Lindbergh's plane we saw that day." John turned to the pilot again. "It was silver and fast and it sounded like ten of your planes all flying together. We saw it when we were at a farm outside of town."

"You know, Bud," the pilot said, "I bet that was Lindbergh and the *Spirit of St. Louis* you saw that day. And maybe someday you'll be just like him."

"A pilot?" John asked, his eyes widening.

"Why not? And maybe a famous pilot, too. You never know."

John and Mr. Glenn thanked the pilot for the ride and headed back to the car.

"I know I don't have to ask you if you had a good time," Mr. Glenn said.

"No sir," John said with a smile. "How about you, Dad? Did you have fun?"

Mr. Glenn thought a moment. "It *was* fun, Bud. But it was more than that. Think about it: When I was your age, the Wright Brothers had only just made their first flight. Nobody thought regular folks like you and me would ever fly. And now people can fly across the oceans! The engineers who design planes keep making them bigger and better. Maybe that's what you'll do someday."

"Make planes?" John asked.

"Why not? You could be anything, son. Study hard. Always do your best. Be curious. You could do anything. You'll be more than a plumber, that's for sure."

"But you're a good plumber, Dad."

18

Mr. Glenn smiled. "I think so, too. But there's so much more out there. Just remember, Bud: Always reach high—as high as you can."

As soon as John got home, he raced over to Hoon's Blacksmith Shop. His friend Rex Hoon was helping his father shoe a horse.

"Mr. Hoon, is it okay if Rex plays for a little while?" John asked.

Mr. Hoon stopped working and wiped his brow. "Sure, why not. I can finish up here."

Rex followed John up the road. "What's up, John?"

"I was just in a plane. A real plane! A biplane. And we flew all over Cambridge and—"

"Get out of here," Rex said, pushing John's shoulder.

"It's true. My dad paid the pilot and he took us up, and we flew, and it was the greatest, best thing I've ever done in my life."

Rex stared at John. "You really did it."

John leaned forward with a huge grin. "Yup."

"Holy cow! John Glenn, you lucky dog! A real plane. Was it a Ryan, like Lucky Lindy's?"

"That's a monoplane—one wing. This was a biplane."

"Oh, yeah." Rex let out a slow whistle. "You flew. Boy, wait till the other guys hear about this. Hey, come on, I'm going to fly, too."

"How?" John asked

"Like this." Rex spread out his arms and ran down the street. "See, I'm not just in a plane, I *am* a plane. Neeeeowwww!" He swooped his arms left and right. "Look, I'm the *Spirit of St. Louis*."

John imitated Rex and ran down the street. "No, *I'm* the *Spirit of St. Louis*," John said, "flying high over the Atlantic Ocean."

The two boys zoomed and zigged and zagged, pretending to fly all around the world. But pretending to fly wasn't much fun for John now. Not after he'd *really* been flying. And he knew someday he would fly again.

Family, Faith, and Country

As the Ohio summer faded into fall, John got ready to go back to school.

"Are you excited, Bud?" his mother asked. She was a bubbly and outgoing woman, with reddish-blond hair. Usually John matched her enthusiasm— but not today.

"I guess," John sighed. "But I'd rather be playing baseball, or going down to Crooked Creek."

"You've had plenty of time for all that," Mrs. Glenn said. "Now it's time for the books."

Mrs. Glenn—Clara—had taught elementary school in Cambridge before John was born. She always reminded him of the importance of a good education.

John liked school, and he did well. But like any eight- or nine-year-old, he liked playing, too. He had lots of friends, like Rex Hoon and Carl Anker and Lloyd White. They played baseball and a game called shinny, which was like field hockey. Sometimes they went into alleys and shot marbles.

John was also friendly with Annie Castor. She was a year older than John, and her father was a dentist. The Castors had moved to New Concord about the same time as the Glenns. The two families spent a lot of time together. John remembered when he was three or so and sharing a playpen with Annie. But as he grew older, he spent most of his time with boys his own age. Annie, though, was still a good friend.

Once school started, John spent his weekdays in class and doing homework and chores—and playing with friends when he could. On

Saturdays, the kids in New Concord headed for the Ohio Valley Dairy, where a sundae topped with nuts cost twenty cents. Sundays were for church and family gatherings.

The Glenns had a strong faith in God. They started each morning with a prayer and a reading from the Bible. The Glenns belonged to the Presbyterian Church. Most people in and around New Concord did, too. The Presbyterians of New Concord were Protestants who followed a strict moral code. They believed good and bad were clearly spelled out in the Bible. The Presbyterian Church had developed in Scotland. Many Scots took their religion with them when they began settling in northern Ireland in the sixteenth and seventeenth centuries. Some of these "Scotch-Irish" Presbyterians then moved on to America.

The towns around New Concord had been founded by Scotch-Irish settlers. New Concord was sometimes called "Saints' Rest," because its citizens were so religious. John had heard from his father about his family's roots in the region and the Glenns' ties to the Presbyterian Church.

"Your great-great grandfather owned a farm near here, back in the eighteen forties. He donated some of his land so the local folks could build the United Presbyterian Church. Same with your mother's family, the Sproats—they were farmers, too. All Scotch-Irish. All Presbyterian. Good people."

"And God-fearing?" John wondered.

"Where did you hear that?" Mr. Glenn asked.

"In Sunday school. The teacher said all good Presbyterians are God-fearing."

Mr. Glenn scratched his head and smiled. "I guess we are, a little bit. But if you follow the Bible and do what you should, then there's not too much to fear. Hard work is important, too. Always work hard, whatever you do. Don't be afraid to succeed."

"Did all the Glenns work hard?"

"Sure, Bud. There wasn't much here when they came to Ohio from Pennsylvania. They had to clear the land and start their farms. They had

24

to help build the towns. But that was one of the things they loved about America—you had the freedom to set out for new places. Explore. Make a good living for you and your family. You could do what you wanted, as long as you didn't hurt anybody else."

"One of our teachers called it 'the American way of life,'" John said.

"I guess that's true," said Mr. Glenn. "Freedom, democracy, doing what's right—that's what our country is all about. Those aren't just words in a book, Bud. And lots of Glenns have been ready to defend that way of life."

"Grandpa Glenn fought in the Civil War, right? For the North?"

"That's right."

"And you fought, too, in nineteen eighteen."

Mr. Glenn fell silent for a moment. "I did, too," he finally replied, half-whispering.

John's father had served in France. Just two weeks after he married Clara Sproat, Mr. Glenn left to fight in the "War to End All Wars"—later known as World War I. He drove trucks that carried shells for the big artillery guns at the front of the battle lines. The deafening roar of exploding shells damaged his hearing. And Mr. Glenn saw how horrible war could be. But the fighting hadn't weakened his belief in the need to defend freedom. John knew his father was proud to have served his country.

In the military, Mr. Glenn learned how to play the bugle, a trumpet without any keys. He bugled reveille, the wake-up song for the troops. He also played taps, the slow, sad song that marked the end of the day—and the burial of a soldier.

New Concord had a town band, and John decided to join. For his instrument, he chose the trumpet. One day, Mr. Glenn came over while John was practicing on his horn. "Hey, Bud, what do you say I teach you a few of my old bugle tunes."

"You still remember those songs?" John asked.

"I'll never forget them," Mr. Glenn answered.

John quickly learned the different military

calls, including taps. His father enjoyed listening to him play.

"You're getting good," Mr. Glenn said.

"Thanks, Dad."

"You know, Decoration Day is coming up."

"Yes sir."

"You know what it's for?"

"It's the day we honor all the American soldiers who were killed fighting wars," John said.

Each year, Mr. Glenn played his bugle during the ceremony for Decoration Day, or Memorial Day. John always stood tall as his father played, the clear notes of his bugle piercing the air.

"I was thinking," Mr. Glenn said, "that maybe this year I could use a little help when I play taps. Maybe you could play along with me."

"You mean it, Dad? You think I'm good enough?"

"Sure, you are. I wouldn't ask if I didn't think you could do it. But you'll have to practice even more now. We'll do it together."

John hugged Mr. Glenn. His father was his

hero, and now he was asking John to do something so important. John was going to help remember the brave men who had fought for the American way of life.

For the next month, John and Mr. Glenn practiced every day. John couldn't think about anything else. Finally, the big day came.

"Are you nervous, Bud?" asked Mrs. Glenn.

"A l-little," John stammered.

His mother smiled. "It's all right to be nervous. You have a big responsibility today. But you can do it."

"Yes, ma'am."

Before on Decoration Day, John had watched the parade with Mrs. Glenn and his little sister, Jean. Once he marched with the town band. But this year, John skipped the parade. He raced by himself over to the cemetery and got ready for his big moment. After a little while he heard the people from the parade gathering in the cemetery.

"Present arms!" a soldier cried. A group of

soldiers raised their rifles.

"Fire!" The guns went off three times. John knew this was a traditional salute to honor the dead. A few seconds passed. Then John heard his father play the first few notes of taps. Mr. Glenn paused. John played the same notes on his trumpet. The song continued this way: First Mr. Glenn played, then John echoed him. Chills ran through John's body as played this mournful tune. Finally, the last few notes from his trumpet rose over the cemetery, then faded away.

Some townspeople came over to thank John for his playing. His father was right behind them.

"Great job, Bud," Mr. Glenn said. "I'm proud of you."

"Thanks, Dad. It was . . . really . . . I don't know . . .

"Moving," Mr. Glenn said. "That's the word. You could feel something in here, couldn't you?" Mr. Glenn tapped John's chest, right over his heart. John nodded.

"There are some things we can't touch with our

hands. We can't see them with our eyes. But we feel them. Things like God and our love for our country. Or like the warm sense you get inside when you do what's right." Mr. Glenn put his arm around John's shoulder. "You remember those feelings, you hear me?"

John looked into his father's eyes. "Yes, sir."

New Heights

On a cold winter morning, John put on his warmest clothes. After school, he and his friends were going sledding.

"You can take that sweater off," Mrs. Glenn said, entering the room. "You're not going anywhere today."

"Why not?" John asked.

"We just heard from the school. There's a scarlet fever epidemic in town. All the elementary school children are supposed to stay inside."

"Yippee! No school!" John shouted.

"And no sledding, either," Mrs. Glenn said. "No going outside at all. It's a quarantine."

John had heard this word often since starting school. Whenever a lot of kids in New Concord got sick with the same disease, the health officials ordered a quarantine. About ten years before, a flu epidemic had hit the United States. Many people, including some of Mrs. Glenn's relatives, had died. Since then, doctors took extra safety steps when a disease, such as scarlet fever, was going around. All the kids, sick and healthy, were ordered inside so the disease wouldn't spread.

"How long will the quarantine last?" John asked.

"They don't know," his mother replied. "But don't worry, we'll find plenty for you to do. I can get you some books from the library."

"Sure, Mom." But John had another idea for how to spend all his new spare time.

"This is a Beech Staggerwing," John explained,

holding up a package. "And this one is a SPAD. The British flew these during World War I."

"Uh-huh," Bob Thompson said. "They just look like a bunch of balsa wood to me." Bob was a cousin of John's from Cambridge. Their parents decided the boys could play together during the quarantine.

"You have to put them together," John said, rolling his eyes. "They're model kits. Haven't you ever made a model before?"

"Once or twice," Bob said. "I don't like the glue much. I stuck my thumb to my forehead once, and it hurt when I pulled it off."

John shook his head. His cousin didn't get it. These weren't just models—they were *planes*. Like the real planes John hoped one day he would build and fly.

"I'll show you how to do it right," John said. "Just watch." He took the pieces of balsa wood for the SPAD (Society for Aviation and Its Derivatives) out of the box. One piece had the outline of the wings and rudder. Another had the fuselage, the body of the plane. With a knife, John carefully followed the outline and cut the pieces out of the wood.

"Now, you take just a little glue," John said, "and put it along the edge, like this." Bob watched closely as John's fingers quickly assembled the pieces. Next John stretched thin, wet paper over the wood. When the paper dried, the plane was complete.

"What's the rubber band for?" Bob asked.

"That's how we make it fly. What's the point of having a plane if you can't fly it? You just turn the propeller, like this." As John turned the prop, the rubber band twisted and became tight. With a few more turns, John stopped and turned to his cousin.

"Ready for takeoff," John said, trying to sound like a real pilot. He held the plane above his head and let go of the propeller.

"It's flying!" Bob cried.

"Sure, it's—"

"And now it's crashing"

34

The boys watched the SPAD's nose drop suddenly. The plane plummeted to the floor. With a jolt, the wings and rudder broke off the plane.

"Now you did it," Bob said, examining the wreckage.

"It's okay," John assured him, picking up the pieces. "It happens all the time."

"What do we do now?"

"Glue it back together and try again."

The boys repaired the plane then took a break for lunch. When they returned to John's room, they prepared for another flight.

"Ready for takeoff," John said again. He released the plane and watched it cross the room.

"It's working," Bob said. "Look at it go!"

The plane rose up and down, then banked as it flew. When the propeller stopped turning, the plane dropped, then bounced to a stop on the ground. It landed upright on its tiny rubber wheels.

"Mission accomplished, General Thompson," John said, saluting his cousin.

"Very good, Major Glenn. You deserve a medal for your heroic flight."

The two boys laughed. Bob turned and picked up a box from the bed. "Okay, let's do the Staggerwing now."

The quarantine dragged on for a few weeks. Bob came back to the Glenns to build models with John. By the time John could go back to school, his room was filled with model planes. He flew them, repaired them when they crashed, then he hung them on string from the ceiling. With every flight, John saw himself working the controls of a real plane, flying higher and faster than any pilot had ever done before.

When spring returned, John went back to his usual routines. Most days after school, he played with his friends. But one day, he went off on his own to explore some nearby woods. He found a huge tree growing near a ravine. The first branch was only a few feet off the ground, so John climbed up. The end of the branch hung out

over the ravine. The bottom of the ravine was at least twenty feet down. Panic hit John like a blast of cold wind. If he fell, he could break a leg—or worse. He crawled back along the branch and climbed down from the tree.

That night, John told his father about his walk in the woods and the tree he found.

"I know which one you mean," Mr. Glenn said. "It's a sycamore. I've seen it when we've been out hunting. And that ravine—it's a pretty good drop."

"Yes, sir," John said. "I got a little, well, a little scared when I was out there."

"Scared, huh?" Mr. Glenn gently took John's shoulders. "You know, Bud, sometimes it's good to be scared. When you're scared, you're feeling fear, and a little fear can keep us from doing some pretty stupid things. But sometimes you need to face your fears. You need to push yourself through whatever is making you scared. That time when we were up in that plane, were you scared?"

"No, sir," John replied. He paused a bit. "Well, maybe a little. But I was more excited than scared."

"And you were up a lot higher than you were on that branch."

"I guess so."

"See, Bud, sometimes fear is just something in your mind. It's what you make of a situation. Think about that the next time you feel a little scared."

The next afternoon, John bolted out of school and headed for the sycamore. He climbed to the branch he had sat on the day before. When he looked out over the ravine, the drop didn't seem so big.

"I can go higher," John whispered to himself.

He pulled himself up a few more branches, then looked down. He must have been thirty feet above the ravine. John's stomach did a little flip-flop. He took a deep breath.

"This isn't so bad," John gulped, trying to reassure himself. He took another breath. His stomach started to steady. "Not so bad at all."

John went up again. He inched out on a branch and looked down into the ravine.

"Hey!" John yelled. "I must be . . . fifty feet high!" The rocks and fallen branches on the bottom of the ravine seemed smaller than ever. John knew that if he fell, he would land on them hard. But John wasn't worried about falling. The fear had flooded from his mind. With a smile, John sat on the branch and looked around. "What a view," he said softly to himself. "Higher is better, that's for sure."

That summer, John sometimes walked into town. He hung out at Hoon's Blacksmith Shop or wandered over to the railroad station. He liked to talk to Mr. Finley, the stationmaster. Mr. Finley knew Morse code, and sometimes he tapped out messages on the telegraph. He also gave instructions to the trains as they passed through New Concord. Mr. Finley would put a message on a hoop attached to the end of a long pole. Without stopping, the train engineers grabbed the hoop as they roared by.

"I bet you could do this, Bud," Mr. Finley said one day. He was getting ready to hand out another message.

"Me? Mr. Finley, you'd let me hold the pole?"

"Sure. You're big enough. Want to give it a try?"

John had watched Mr. Finley hold the pole dozens of times, but he couldn't imagine doing it himself. What if he dropped the pole? What if the train ripped the pole from his hands—and took his arm along, too? But before he could think too much, John nodded yes.

John came next to Mr. Finley on the platform. The stationmaster handed him the pole. "The train's coming in from the west, from Norwich," said Mr. Finley. "She'll be going about fifty or sixty miles per hour. The engineer will be ready for you, but you have to keep that pole steady, you understand?"

"Yes sir," John answered. He gripped the pole

tightly in both hands, and Mr. Finley went back to the station.

John heard the train first: a distant, high whistle. The sound grew louder. Then John could see the train, its locomotive coughing puffs of black smoke. As the train neared the station, John could feel its rumble through his feet. He thought he had never seen a bigger, faster train in his life. It seemed to be pointing straight at him, like a huge black arrow. John fought to keep his eyes open and his feet on the platform.

"Can't let him see I'm scared," John said to himself. "Can't let Mr. Finley down. Just hold on."

The train roared toward the station. It didn't slow for a second. John held his breath, then felt a tug as the engineer grabbed the hoop at the end of the pole. The wind from the rushing train staggered John, but he didn't lose his grip. In a flash, the train was past the station.

"Good job, Bud," Mr. Finley said. He took the pole and went back to his office. John watched

42

the train turn into a small black dot in the distance. This was another test, he thought, another test about fear. And John knew he had passed.

The Ohio Rangers

John and his friend Lloyd White studied the book in front of them. It sat on an egg crate that the boys had flipped over to use as a table.

"Let's check how to make a slipknot," Lloyd suggested.

"We know all the knots," John said. "Go to the part about merit badges."

Lloyd flipped through the pages. "Don't you wish we could really be Boy Scouts?"

"Yeah, that would be great," John said. "Building fires, camping in the woods. Why'd we get stuck in a town that doesn't have a troop?"

"Yeah."

The boys stared at the Boy Scout handbook in front of them.

"Wait a minute," John piped up. "Who says we can't have our own Scout troop?"

"Huh?"

"Sure. We can have our own group. We just won't call it the Boy Scouts—it'll be something else. But we'll still follow the handbook and do all the things real Scouts do. And we can have the meetings right here—if your dad says it's okay."

The boys were in a small room above Mr. White's family business, a hatchery. Downstairs, chickens laid eggs. The eggs then went into incubators, where they hatched. The warmth of the incubators drifted up into the room above. So did the smell of chickens, but John barely noticed it.

"I think Pop would go along," Lloyd said. "And I know some guys at school who will want to join."

"Me too. Let's try to get them together for a

meeting next week."

"We need a name," Lloyd said. "We have to tell people who we are."

John thought for a moment. "How about . . . the Rangers? The Ohio Rangers."

Lloyd smiled. "The Ohio Rangers. Sounds good."

"This meeting of the Ohio Rangers will now come to order."

John stood in front of a group of boys. The Rangers had held their first official meeting in October 1932. John was everyone's choice to be the club's first president. Now it was June, and the Rangers were making plans for the summer.

"We've got a ball game next week with a team from Norwich," Lloyd said.

"And I talked to Mr. Waller at the movie theater," said George Roy. "He'll sell us tickets for ten cents a piece, and then we can sell them for the usual price—fifteen cents."

"A nickel profit on every ticket," John said.

"With that and our dues, we should have plenty of money."

The boys nodded and discussed how they would use their treasury.

"Okay, Rangers," John interrupted. "There's still one more thing. What about camping out?"

George spoke up again. "I saw a good spot near my house. It looks out over Crooked Creek. It's flat, and there's a good clearing for the tents. My dad says it's okay if we use it."

"What do you think, Mr. Keck?" John asked.

Reiss Keck was a teacher at the elementary school. He had agreed to be the Rangers' adviser. He helped them follow all the rules a real Boy Scout troop used. Mr. Keck came to most meetings, but he let John run them. Now, he stood up to speak. "I think it sounds great. But remember, Rangers—having a campsite will take a lot of work. It's going to be your responsibility to keep it up. Are you sure you're up for it?"

John looked out at the Rangers. He could see they were as excited as he was about the camp.

"We're sure, Mr. Keck," he said.

"Then let's get at it!"

The boys stampeded out of their clubhouse and headed for the site. John looked around and realized George was right—the spot was perfect.

"We can have paths here," John said, motioning with his hand. "And the tents can go over there. And in the middle, we can have a flagpole." He looked up at Mr. Keck. "Does that sound good?"

The young man smiled. "You don't have to ask me, John. Check with the other Rangers. This is their site, too. But I think the guys will go along with you. They picked you as president for a good reason, you know."

John felt good hearing Mr. Keck say that. But he didn't spend too much time enjoying the compliment—there was too much work to do.

That afternoon, and for the next few days, the boys cleared out branches and rocks. They used the rocks as borders along walkways. A few of the Rangers went to the local lumberyard and hauled back bags of sawdust. They made a large circle with the dust, where the boys would march, like soldiers in a drill. When the Rangers were finally done, John looked around.

"I bet there isn't a Boy Scout troop in Ohio with a better campsite than this." The other Rangers cheered.

That summer, John's life revolved around the Rangers and their campsite. Almost every day, when he finished his chores, he bolted over to the site. Usually a few other Rangers were already there, playing or relaxing in the sun. When it got too hot, the boys ran down to the creek and dived into its cool, rushing water.

At dinnertime, the Rangers built a campfire and brought out hamburgers and hot dogs. John usually put a hot dog on a stick and roasted it over the flames. When sunset came, the boys gathered around the flagpole.

"Rangers," John cried out, "salute!"

The boys saluted as the flag came down the pole for the night. Then it was time for the boys to climb into their small canvas tents. John took out his trumpet and played taps. In the morning, the boys headed home for their chores, then headed back to the camp. On more than one starlit night, John turned to Lloyd with a smile. "You know, summer doesn't get any better than this."

"H-hel-l-lo, John."

"Hi, Annie."

John watched Annie Castor get off her bike. She approached him as he stepped out the front door. John still thought of Annie as one of his best friends—even if she was a girl.

"I-I d-d-on't see mu-much of you anymore."

"I'm busy now, Annie. I'm president of the Rangers."

"I kn-know."

Annie spoke with a stutter. Some of the kids at school sometimes snickered when she spoke, until John told them to cut it out. He couldn't stand that kind of cruelty, especially to someone he'd known almost his whole life. John hardly noticed the stutter anymore. "I'm kind of in a rush, Annie. I'm going out to the campsite."

"Th-that's why I stopped by. You know I'm in the G-Girl Scouts?"

"Yeah."

"My troop was wo-wondering . . . "

"Yeah?"

"C-could we b-b-borrow your campsite for a night?"

John fought back a laugh. "You *girls* want to sleep out in the woods? By yourselves?"

Annie nodded.

"But what about the bears, and the lions, and the other spooky stuff out there?" John came closer to Annie and made a scary face. "Oooooooooooo!"

Annie did not flinch. "If they hav-haven't scared y-you boys off, they won't b-b-bother us. And there are n-n-no lions in Ohio."

"You'll see," John taunted.

"S-so what do you s-s-say?"

"I'll have to check with the other Rangers,"

John said. "I'll let you know tomorrow."

"Girls at our campsite? No way!"

The other Rangers shouted their approval as Lloyd spoke.

"This a Ranger site, for Rangers only!"

"Yeah!"

"Okay, I get it, okay." John tried to quiet them down. "What do you think, Mr. Keck?"

The boys looked over to their adviser, who had come out to the camp for this emergency meeting.

"You're right, Lloyd. This is your site. You made it what it is."

The Rangers murmured their agreement.

"But, as Rangers, you also have a duty to help others. And to be courteous. Aren't those the rules you agreed to follow?"

The boys looked at each other, a little dejected. This was not what they wanted to hear.

"Yes sir," John finally said.

"I think letting the Girl Scouts stay here would

be a very generous gesture," Mr. Keck said. "It's only one night."

"I guess we should take a vote," John said. "All those in favor of letting the"—he took a deep breath—"Girl Scouts stay here, say aye."

A round of weak "ayes" answered John.

"The vote is passed," John said. "But just one night!"

Annie and her troop chose the next Saturday for their sleep over. That night, John lay in bed, tossing and turning. It felt strange to feel the mattress beneath him, not the gentle lumps of the earth. He imagined the Girl Scouts giggling at dumb jokes or playing with dolls, or whatever it was girls did at sleep overs.

Outside the house, trees rustled in the wind. A few drops of rain hit the window in John's room. Then a few more streaked the glass. Within a minute, the rain poured down. John saw a flash of white light, then heard the boom of thunder.

"Some storm," John said to himself. He got up to close the window. As he climbed back into bed, he thought of just one thing: how the camp would be through the storm.

In the morning, John got up and looked out the window. The sky was blue and clear. John dressed and rushed through the house. "I'll have breakfast later," he called to his mother. "I've got to check out the camp."

Some of the other Rangers had the same idea. John was not the first one to get there. A few of the boys and Mr. Keck were looking over the empty site.

"What happened?" John asked. "Where are the girls?"

"Their parents came and got them last night," Mr. Keck explained.

John saw that the sawdust had washed away. The canvas tents sat in a soggy pile. Mud covered almost the whole site.

"They left the camp?" John asked in disbelief. "Because of a little storm?"

"Little?" Mr. Keck said. "That thunderstorm was one of the worst to hit New Concord in years. And what would they have done if they had stayed?"

"Maybe they could have done something about this," John said. He motioned to the mess around him. "Look at the camp!" As he surveyed the damage, John felt as if someone had walloped him in the stomach.

"Is that all you care about, John?" Mr. Keck asked. "What about the girls' safety?"

John didn't have an answer.

"And this camp is not the whole universe, you know. This is not the end of the world."

John flushed a bit. He could tell he was acting like a baby.

"Yeah, John, it's no big deal," Lloyd said. "We'll find another spot. Besides, the summer is almost over."

John waded through the mud. He thought about all the work the Rangers had done. But they could do it again, if they had to. And Mr. Keck was probably right: There was more to life than being an Ohio Ranger.

Tough Times

"Mom," John called out. "There's another one at the door."

Mrs. Glenn hurried out of the kitchen and came to the front door. Outside, a young man stood on the steps, a ragged hat in his hand.

"Don't say 'another one,'" whispered Mrs. Glenn. "He's a man, not a thing."

John glanced out at the man and his unshaven face. "Yes, ma'am."

Mrs. Glenn smiled at the man. "Can I help you sir?"

"Well, uh, you see, ma'am . . . " The man stared down at his worn brown shoes, searching for his words. John noticed the holes in his pants and the small, scuffed suitcase at his feet. A piece of rope held the case together. "You see, ma'am, I'm a little down on my luck, and—"

"And you were wondering if I could spare some food," Mrs. Glenn finished for him.

The man looked at her. His eyes seemed to fill with tears. "That's it, ma'am, that's it exactly. It's nothing I'm proud to do, you understand, but I haven't eaten—"

Mrs. Glenn helped up her hand. "Please— don't say another word. What's your name?"

"Roy. Roy Atkins."

"Well, Roy Atkins, come on in. John will show you to the kitchen."

Roy wiped his eyes, and a smile touched his lips. "Thank you, ma'am, thank you. Not everyone will help out a bum."

"Oh, I don't help out bums, either," Mrs. Glenn said. "But someone who's down on his luck—that's another story. But you should know, Roy, I don't give handouts."

Roy looked puzzled. "Ma'am?"

"After I get you something to eat, I'd like you to help do a little weeding in the garden."

"Of course, ma'am. Wouldn't be no trouble at all."

"That's what you think," John said. "Wait till you see our garden. And usually I have to weed the whole thing by myself."

Mrs. Glenn smiled as she followed John and Roy through the house. "Yes, our Bud's turning into quite a farmer."

"Farmer," John said with a hint of disgust. "That's not what I want to be."

"So what do you want to be someday?" Roy asked.

"A pilot. I want to fly. I'm going to save all my money so I can take flying lessons, and then go to Columbus and get into a Waco biplane, and—"

"That's still a few years off," Mrs. Glenn interrupted. "In the meantime, learning a little farming won't hurt. Even pilots have to eat. And so does our guest. Come on, get Roy settled with a plate and some silverware."

Roy wasn't the first stranger to show up at the Glenns' doorstep looking for a meal. John had seen these men for the last few years, since the start of the Great Depression. In October 1929, the stock market collapsed. Many Americans who had invested their money in companies lost their wealth. The economy soured, and as time went on, millions of people lost their jobs. Families lost their homes. John knew of children in New Concord who had been forced to live with relatives far away. Men like Roy trudged across the country, looking for any work they could find. If they couldn't find a job, they counted on the kindness of people like Mrs. Glenn.

John and his family had it better than most people. Mr. Glenn still had the plumbing business, though he didn't make as much money as he did before the Depression started. He also started a new business—selling cars. But not many people could afford a car when they could barely buy food for their families.

The Glenns helped themselves by starting a garden. Mr. Glenn dug up a plot of land next to his shop, then another by their house. Later, he rented two acres of land across the street. The family garden was now more like a small farm, with corn, potatoes, peas, and many other crops. John spent long hours weeding, hoeing, and picking so the Glenns would have plenty of food on the table.

"Now Roy," Mrs. Glenn said, "I have some leftover roast beef and mashed potatoes. And do you like carrots?"

"Whatever you have, ma'am, is fine with me," Roy replied.

"Do you need me for anything right now?" John asked his mother. She didn't look up as she prepared the food for their guest.

"No, Bud. Why don't you start out on your rounds."

"Thanks, Mom. I'll be home before dark."

John headed outside and went over to his wooden wagon. It was already loaded with bunches of rhubarb, another crop from the Glenns' garden. To make money, John sold the rhubarb in his neighborhood. The pink stalks of the rhubarb were a tart treat. He went to his first stop, the Grimms' house.

"Well, it's John Glenn, the rhubarb man."

"Hello, Mrs. Grimm. I've got lots of fresh rhubarb today, all cut and washed and ready to cook."

"It does look good," she said. Mrs. Grimm was John's best customer. She picked a few bunches out of the wagon and handed him a few coins.

"Thanks, Mrs. Grimm." John wheeled the wagon down the sidewalk, looking for another customer. He rolled it down toward Muskingum, the local college. His mother had gone to school there. Before the Depression, the school started building a new gym. When the economy went bad, construction stopped. Now just a steel skeleton stood on the site, waiting for walls and a roof. Every time John saw that half-finished building, he remembered how tough things were all over the country. He felt lucky his family still had so much.

One night in the spring of 1933, John spread out on the living room couch. The Glenns had just finished dinner. John tried to read a book, but he kept hearing his parents' voices rising from the kitchen. They tried to whisper, but John could still tell they were worried about something. He got up and inched toward the kitchen doorway.

John saw his father sitting at the table. All around him were pieces of paper covered with numbers.

"Clara," Mr. Glenn said to his wife, "I'm afraid we're going to lose the house."

John dropped the book he held in his hand. His parents turned and saw him in the doorway. "Wh-what's going to happen to us?" John asked in a hoarse whisper.

"John!" Mrs. Glenn said. "You shouldn't be listening to this."

"No, no, Clara, it's all right," Mr. Glenn said softly. "He's old enough to know what's at stake. Come here, Bud."

John moved toward the table.

"Do you know what a mortgage is?" Mr. Glenn asked.

"It's something you get when you buy a house," John said.

"That's right. It's a loan. The bank loaned us money so we could buy the house. We have to pay back the money, plus a little extra, before we actually own the house. Well, you know, the banks aren't doing so well these days."

John nodded. "We talked about it in school."

"So now our bank is coming to people like us and trying to collect more of the money it's owed. But right now things are tight for us. I don't know if we'll be able to pay the money."

"I can sell more rhubarb," John offered. "Or wash cars. I've made money before washing cars."

Mr. Glenn smiled. "I know you're a hard worker, Bud. But all that still wouldn't be enough."

John looked deeply into his father's eyes. "Will you send me and Jean away? Will we have to live with someone else?"

"Bud, we would never send you away. This family will always stick together."

"But, Bud," Mrs. Glenn cut in, "things will be tough for a while."

"Yes, ma'am."

For the next few weeks the Glenns scraped together all the money they could. The bank gave them some extra time to pay on the loan. But even with money so tight, there was one thing Mr. Glenn would not give up. He made plans for the family's annual trip to Columbus for the Ohio State Fair. John loved the animals and the science exhibits and the food. And a trip to Columbus meant another special treat—a stop at the airport.

"Momma, why do we always go to the airport?" Jean asked.

"Because your brother enjoys it, hon."

"But the planes just go up in the air, or they

come down. They don't *do* anything."

John tried to be patient with his littler sister. After all, she was only six. "See, Jeanie, flying isn't easy. Engineers have to work real hard to get a plane into the air. And the pilot has to study a long time before he can fly one. And, don't you see, being up in the sky is so wonderful!"

"It looks boring," Jean said.

"Well, it's not," John said, watching another Beech rumble up into the sky. "It's a dream come true. To leave the ground and soar through the air . . . I did it once, you know, with Dad. And I'm gonna do it again."

"Besides," Mr. Glenn said, "taking your brother to the airport is cheaper than going to a movie. It's entertainment that doesn't cost us a cent!"

Since March 1933, a new president had led the United States. Franklin Roosevelt had told the American people he would try to end the Depression and put people back to work. Until then, he said, the government would spend money to help people in need. One summer day in 1934, Mr. Glenn came home smiling. "He's done it," Mr. Glenn said. "He's done it."

"Who's done what?" Mrs. Glenn asked.

"The president. He set up a new program to help people pay their mortgages. People like us. We should be all right."

"We're gonna keep the house?" John asked.

"Yes, sir, Bud, we sure are." Mr. Glenn sat down and gave John a hug. "Now, you might know, I don't always care for Mr. Roosevelt. And I believe people need to take care of themselves. It's called self-reliance. Your mother and I have tried to teach you to be self-reliant."

"Yes, sir."

"But, sometimes, Bud, people can't take care of themselves no matter how hard they try. And when that happens, sometimes they need a hand. Your mother does it for the men who come to the door. And the government just did it for us. There's no shame in taking that help when you really need it."

John had never thought much about the government in Washington, D.C. It seemed so far away from New Concord. But now he realized the important role it could play for people like him and his parents. And someday John hoped to pay back his country for the help it gave.

New Lessons

"Hey, John, I hear you're going out for the Student Council."

"That's right." John didn't see who had called to him. He kept walking down the polished hallway of New Concord High School. He smiled and chatted with friends as he passed. It was September 1935, the start of John's first year at the school. Already he had a full schedule.

"Got your article for the school paper?" someone asked.

"Right here," John said, holding up his notebook.

"Don't forget band practice tomorrow," one girl called.

"I know."

"Hey, Glenn, see ya at football practice," a beefy student said.

"I'll be there," John said.

Turning a corner, John saw Annie Castor leaning against her locker. She was talking to some friends. She smiled as he approached. Annie was a sophomore, but she never treated John as if he were a year younger.

"H-hi, John," she said.

"Hey, Annie," John said with a wave. He turned to the other girls. "Hello." The girls smiled and looked at Annie. John was already turning from just some redheaded kid into a good-looking young man.

"Did you have fun at the movies last week?" John asked Annie.

"Of c-c-course. We sh-should g-go again."

"Sure, I'd like that. Well, I gotta run."

"Where're you going, John?" one of the girls asked.

"Civics class."

"Ugh," the girl said. "Mr. Steele. That's just what he is—steely, all cold and hard."

"Nah, he's not so bad," John said. "Not if you work hard and pay attention."

"A-and you *always* d-d-do," Annie teased.

"Oh," her friend said, "so John's a *brain*."

John felt his cheeks start to burn. "I don't know what you mean by that. I like school. And I study hard. That's how you can make something of yourself."

"And what do you want to make of yourself?" another girl asked.

"I dunno. Maybe a scientist. Or an engineer."

"Or a p-pilot?" Annie asked.

The bell rang. Students in the hallway began running to class.

"Gotta go," John said. "Talk to you later, Annie. Bye, girls."

John zigged and zagged through the other

students rushing to their classes. He didn't want to be late for Mr. Steele's class. John zipped through the classroom door just as it was starting to close. On the other side of it was Mr. Steele.

"Glad you could make it, Mr. Glenn."

"Yes, sir," John said, quickly taking his seat. He settled in and took out his note cards. Mr. Steele made all his students take notes on their class work and readings. Then they could study from their cards before a test.

Mr. Steele paced back and forth in front of the room. He held a small rubber ball in his hand. He squeezed the ball as he paced, occasionally switching it from one hand to the other. "All right," he finally said. "Who can tell me about the U.S. Senate? What is it, what does it do?"

John shot up his hand.

"John?"

"The U.S. Senate is one of the two houses of the U.S. Congress. Each state has two senators, for a total of ninety-six.* Each member serves a six-year term."

"Good," Mr. Steele said. "What else?"

John took a breath and went on. "The Senate, along with the House of Representatives, makes laws for the country. The Senate also approves treaties signed with foreign countries and approves the president's appointments, like cabinet members and judges."

"Excellent, John. I can see you've done the reading."

John did his best work in math and science, but he liked civics, too. Mr. Steele made politics and history come to life. John liked learning about how the government worked. He always remembered Mr. Steele's lecture about the political duties of an American.

"When you turn twenty-one," Mr. Steele said, "you earn one of the greatest rights in the world—the right to vote. You choose who will represent you. That's what politicians do—represent your interests. They serve *you*. And holding

*At the time, there were only forty-eight states. Alaska and Hawaii both became states in 1959.

a public office is a great responsibility. If you ever run for an office, you have to deserve it. You have to have character. You know what that means, John?"

"Being honest, and doing what's right for everybody, not just yourself."

"That's it. Now, maybe you'll never run for president, or senator. But you can still get involved at some level. And you can vote in every election, no matter how small."

John's dad had served on the New Concord school board. He liked to tell John, "See, even somebody with a sixth-grade education can be a politician. Think how far you could go, Bud, if you study hard."

Freshman year went on, and John did well in school. He liked his classes, and he played three sports: football, basketball, and tennis. The next year went well, too. As his sophomore year was about to end, John received a visit from an old friend, Reiss Keck.

74

"Hello, Mr. Keck." John said. "It's been a while."

"It sure has, John. You know, you can call me Reiss now, if you'd like."

"Okay, Mr. Keck."

The older man laughed. "I don't see many of you boys anymore since the Rangers broke up."

"Yeah," John said. "It was tough keeping them together, once we got older. Too many other things to do."

"I understand," Reiss said. "You probably have a lot to do this summer, too."

John nodded. "Working for my dad, in the plumbing business."

"Do you think he'd be willing to spare you for a few weeks?"

"What do you mean, Mr. Keck?"

"My sister Ferida and I are planning a little car trip. We're going to head up to Canada, then drive down through New England. I thought you might enjoy coming along."

John couldn't believe it. A car trip—without

his parents! On the road for hours every day, seeing new places. What an opportunity. "I don't know Mr. Keck, but I sure would like to go. I'll ask tonight and let you know."

That night at dinner, John told his parents about seeing Mr. Keck.

"Such a nice young fella," Mr. Glenn said. "What's he up to this summer?"

"Well, he and his sister are taking a trip up to Canada."

"In that Chevy I sold him?" Mr. Glenn asked. "Good for them. They'll have fun. That Chevy runs like a charm."

John swallowed. "Yes, sir. And Dad—they want me to go with them."

"A car trip to Canada?" Mrs. Glenn said. "How nice of Mr. Keck to ask."

"You mean you think it's a good idea?" John asked.

"Why not?" Mr. Glenn said. "You're almost an adult. Time to get away from us for a change. And Reiss is a good man. It'll be good for you."

"What about the business?" John asked.

"I'll get by. Besides, there'll be plenty of the summer left when you get back."

Within a few days, all the plans were set. When school ended, John and the Kecks loaded their bags into Reiss's Chevy.

"Looking forward to seeing all the sites?" Ferida asked.

"Sure," John replied. "I love traveling. Going somewhere, being on the move—it's great."

Their first stop was Youngstown, Ohio. Reiss wanted to take John to see a steel plant. Inside, John watched huge metal kettles pour out rivers of red, liquid steel. Sparks flew in all directions.

"What do you think?" Reiss asked.

"I've never seen anything like it!" John said.

"That's was this trip is about," Reiss said. "Exploring new things."

At Niagara Falls, New York, they went to see an electric plant. The water at the falls turned enormous turbines to create energy. In Canada, Reiss drove to the banks of the St. Lawrence River.

"Could we go for a swim?" John asked.

"I don't know, John," Reiss said. "It's a little early for swimming up here. The ice just melted not too long ago."

"That's all right. It won't be too cold for me."

"Are you sure?" Ferida asked.

"Positive. I swim in cold water all the time back home." John changed into his trunks in the back of the car. He sprinted out and dived into the river.

"How is it?" Reiss inquired.

"It, it's ok-k-k-kay," John chattered. "J-just a little chilly."

"Oh, just a little," Reiss said with a smile.

"Yeah. But I think I've had enough." John jumped out of the river. He shook his arms and legs, trying to get warm.

"Don't tell John Glenn he can't do something, hmm?" Ferida said. "That just makes him more determined to try."

John wrapped a blanket around his shivering body. "I guess so. But I did it. Not many guys in

New Concord can say they swam in the St. Lawrence River."

From Canada, John and the Kecks headed for Boston. They stopped at the USS *Constitution*— "Old Ironsides." From his history class, John remembered how the sailors on the ship fought so bravely during the War of 1812.

The next stop was New York, and the three travelers rode a ferry out to the Statue of Liberty. In Philadelphia, they saw the Liberty Bell.

"This is like seeing all of America's history on one trip," John said.

"And can you feel it?" Reiss asked.

"What?"

"It's like a presence. Like all those great Revolutionary leaders are standing right here."

The trip across Pennsylvania to New Concord wasn't too long. At home, John thanked Reiss and Ferida for asking him to go.

"I hope you learned something, John," Reiss said.

John nodded. "And not just about steel

plants and generators and history."

"What's else?"

"When you want to find out about something, you have to go out and experience it for yourself. Challenge yourself."

Reiss smiled. "And I bet you have a few more challenges in store before you're all through."

The Cruiser

"What do you think, Annie? Isn't she a beauty?"

John walked all around the car. He patted its rusty red sides and tapped on its spotted windshield.

Annie examined the car. "I guess it's all r-r-right," she finally said. "It n-n-needs some w-w-work."

"Sure, its needs some work. This car has been through a lot. But it runs. And it'll run even better when I'm done with it."

"W-w-what is it?" Annie asked.

"A twenty-nine Chevy roadster. Look, it even has a rumble seat in the back." John walked behind the Chevy. He showed Annie the seat that popped up from the rear of the car.

"Uh-huh," Annie said, trying to sound interested.

"My dad got it as a trade-in. He says I can drive it as much as I want. It's kinda like a birthday present, for turning sixteen."

The Chevy was a convertible. Its cloth roof was ragged with holes. The car had sputtered and bucked all the way to Annie's house, but John knew he could fix that. It wasn't like flying a plane, John knew. But having his own car would give him the freedom and speed he craved.

"I'm going to call it the Cruiser," John said. "Sounds good, doesn't it?"

"I s-s-suppose. But why that?"

"Because when it's all done, I'm going to go cruising all over. And you'll come, too, won't you Annie?"

Annie smiled. "Y-you mean me and the r-r-rest

of your friends? Or j-just me?"

"Well, ah, both, I guess," John stammered. "But just you, when we can."

John and Annie weren't just childhood friends anymore. They were a couple. Annie's friends sometimes teased that if Annie was around, John had to be close by. Annie and John already felt they would always be together.

But for the next few weeks, Annie didn't see much of John. He was too busy with the Cruiser. First he sanded down the old faded paint and put on a new coat of red. Then he ripped off the convertible roof. He put a canvas tarp in the car, to cover the seats when it rained. John also drilled holes in the floor so any rain that did get in would drain out. Next John got the engine running as well as he could. Finally, the Cruiser was ready for a test drive.

John picked up Lloyd White, and they drove all over New Concord. After about half an hour, John pulled over.

"What's wrong?" Lloyd asked.

"The radiator," John explained. He pulled a jug of water out of the back seat. "It has a leak that I can't fix. I have to keep adding more water."

"Nice car, Glenn," Lloyd teased.

"Where's yours, White? I don't see your twenty-nine Chevy roadster."

"Hey, speaking of water . . . "

"Yeah?"

"The practice field got soaked in that rain last night," Lloyd said. "I was down there this morning. It's nothing but mud."

"So?"

"So maybe you should see what kind of traction this thing has," Lloyd said.

"Take the Cruiser through mud?" John asked in disbelief.

"Why not? It'll wash off. 'Course, that paint job of yours might wash off, too."

"I don't know, Lloyd. Going through mud—"

"What's the matter? You don't think this jalopy can make it?"

John stared at Lloyd, then cracked a slight

smile. "Are you daring my car? Are you daring *me?*"

Without waiting for a reply, John jumped over the closed door and into the driver's seat. He put the Chevy in gear and roared off toward Crooked Creek. The high school's football practice field was next to the creek. After strong rains, the creek ran over its banks and flooded the field. Lloyd was right—the field was now a sea of mud.

"You ready?" John asked.

"Let 'er rip."

John floored the gas pedal, and the Cruiser sped forward. When the car reached the mud, its wheels began to spin. John managed to keep the Chevy moving forward. He cut the wheel hard to left, and the car spun like a top.

"Doughnut!" the boys shouted as mud sprayed from the wheels. John turned the steering wheel the other way, and the Cruiser started to whirl in the other direction.

"You can really drive this thing!" Lloyd called out.

"No problem," John said. "I've had my license

since I was fifteen. Driving is a piece of—"

The Cruiser shook. The boys felt the car hit something hard. John slammed on the brakes, and the car's rear end swiveled left and right. Finally the Cruiser stopped in the middle of the mud.

"That didn't sound good," Lloyd said.

"Nope."

John got of the car. He trudged through the mud and bent down to look under the front end.

"Oh, great!"

"What?" Lloyd asked.

"We hit a log. It's still stuck under here." John struggled to pull the log free. "And I think I took out the oil pan. I can see some oil leaking."

"Think you can get home all right?"

"Yeah. I just hope I can fix it without my dad noticing."

John could do a lot of things with the Cruiser. But fixing a broken oil pan without his father noticing was not one of them.

"Consider yourself grounded," said Mr.

Glenn. He looked over the muddy Chevy.

"Yes, sir," John said.

"And don't expect me to help you fix this."

"No, sir."

"I hope you learned your lesson," Mr. Glenn added. "No more joyriding in the fields."

"Yes, sir."

John soon got the Cruiser back on the road. He took Annie out for ice cream, or gave her rides home from school. And he kept his word to his father: He never took the car off the road again. But John still wanted to test the limits of what he could do in the Cruiser. The Chevy wasn't fast, but John could still find some excitement behind the wheel. Some afternoons, he took the car to the New Concord railroad bridge.

The bridge was narrow, just wide enough for one car to pass. The road arched up steeply over the railroad tracks below. Once he was on the bridge, John couldn't see if another car was approaching. To the boys at New Concord High, barreling over the road at top speed was called "shooting the bridge." John was one of the most daring "shooters" of all.

One day as John and Annie were going home, they crossed the railroad bridge. John drove carefully along the road.

"No sh-shooting today?" Annie asked.

"What do you mean, Annie?"

"J-J-John, I hear the b-b-boys talking. They say you sh-shoot the bridge."

"Well, maybe once or twice."

"B-b-but, it's so d-dangerous," Annie said. Her dark eyes looked frightened.

"You sound like my mother," John said. "It's not so dangerous. Besides, it's fun."

"What m-m-makes it so fun?"

John thought about what he felt as he roared across the bridge. "Because you're going as fast as you can. And the road is so skinny, you think you might not fit. And you hit the top of the hill and, just for a second, you're in the air! It's like you're flying—just for a second, anyway. I guess there's a little danger. You don't know what's waiting for you on the other side of the hill. But that's part of the thrill."

"Thrill! You could get killed!" Annie seemed to fight back a tear.

"Oh, Annie, it's all right. I know how to drive. I won't get hurt."

A few days later, John drove by himself to the railroad bridge. He sat in the Cruiser at the bottom of the small hill.

"Captain Glenn, ready for takeoff," he said to himself. He saw himself as the pilot of a Gee Bee racing plane. He gunned the motor of the Cruiser and sped up the hill. At the top, he felt the car leave the ground. John rose out of his seat. He thought that if he let go of the wheel he'd fly off into space. Then, he and the car returned to earth. John let out a "whoop," his heart beating wildly. But his face hardened as saw another car coming up the other side of the bridge.

John knew he was going too fast to stop. He had no room to turn. He saw the driver of the other car. It was an older man. John didn't recognize him. The man hit his brakes and swerved. The Cruiser barely scraped past. When John got back to the main road, he stopped. The other car was gone. John felt the sweat pouring down his face. "That," he finally said to himself, "was too close."

He sat for a moment, then headed down the road. He stopped by Annie's house. "I made a decision today," John told her.

"What?"

"You're right. It's kinda stupid to shoot the bridge. I'm never going to do it again."

Annie smiled.

"But you have to know, Annie, I'm always going to want excitement. I'm always going to try new things."

"I kn-n-now."

"I don't see myself running my father's plumbing business, or selling cars."

"I kn-now," Annie repeated, almost in a whisper.

"If we stay together"—John felt his face flush a bit—"if we stay together, you have to accept who I am. I'm not afraid of danger."

"I know." Annie took John's hand and smiled. "That's one r-reason why I l-like you so much."

Off to the Races

As high school went on, John crammed his days with activities. He played his three sports and continued to study hard for his classes. He also played trumpet in the town band, and he and Annie joined the school's singing group. In his junior year, John was elected president of his class. His classmates appreciated his intelligence and leadership skills. But with all his responsibilities, John still found time to think about flying. He tried to keep planes a part of his life.

Each year, New Concord High School held a

banquet for the junior and senior classes. The dinner featured skits and speeches by the students. In the spring of 1938, John helped plan the event. When he met with the other class officers who were involved, he made a suggestion. "Let's give this year's banquet an aviation theme."

"Aviation?" one girl said. "You mean airplanes?"

"Sure," John replied. "Ohio was the longtime home of the Wright Brothers. And planes are really taking off."

"Very funny," another girl said. "Planes are taking off."

John made a face, not realizing his joke. "Come on, I'm serious. Look at the Pan Am clippers."

"What are they?" one boy asked.

"The clippers are the biggest and best passenger planes ever built. They're like cruise ships with wings. Pretty soon you'll be able to fly them all over the world."

"Maybe *you* can," the boy said. "But I'll never

afford a plane flight like that."

"Flying is getting cheaper all the time," John argued. "And safer, too. I bet every one of us will fly somewhere in a plane within the next ten or fifteen years."

"When are you going to fly, John?" another boy asked.

"I've already flown—once. Well, just for a short ride. When I was a kid. But someday I'm going to get my pilot's license and fly wherever I want."

The other students shook their heads. They didn't share John's enthusiasm for planes. And they weren't sure they wanted aviation as theme for the banquet.

But John didn't give up. "Aviation is about the future," he said. "It's about going new places and doing new things. And that's what the seniors will do when they graduate. And for us juniors, we're going to soar off to new experiences, too, when we become seniors. Aviation is the perfect theme."

John won his argument. He convinced the officers to accept his idea. At the junior-senior banquet, the students received a program. On the cover was a picture of a Ford plane. The title was, "NCHS Senior Airways. Dependable, safe service." John, as one of the hosts for the evening, was called the pilot.

The school year ended soon after the banquet. John found a job at a summer camp run by the YMCA. He set off in the Cruiser, ready to make pit stops to add more water to the leaky radiator. He spent the summer serving food to 125 young campers.

When he came home to New Concord, his father had a surprise for him. "Ready to take a little trip before school starts?" Mr. Glenn asked.

"Okay, Dad," John said. Where are we going?"

"It's a surprise. But get your camping gear ready. Your uncle Ralph and cousin Bob are going, too. We're leaving tomorrow."

The two young men and their fathers set out late the next morning. John prodded his father and uncle for information about the trip. They just laughed.

"You have to figure it out, Bud," said Uncle Ralph. "You're a smart guy, you'll get it."

John watched the road signs as they drove north. They passed Canton, then Akron. Finally John realized where they were going. "Cleveland!" he cried. "The National Air Races!"

"And you know who will be there, don't you?" Uncle Ralph asked.

John nodded. "Roscoe Turner."

"Who's he?" Bob asked.

"You've never heard of Roscoe Turner?" John said in disbelief. "The American Speed King? He's about the most famous pilot in the world. During the war, he served on balloons and then became a pilot. Afterward, he became a barnstormer—traveling the country and doing stunts. He travels around with a pet lion cub."

"Is he crazy?" Robert asked.

John smiled. "Nah. Just . . . different. He's like a movie star, with his big mustache. And he wears a blue suit and black leather boots."

"He's a racer, too," Mr. Glenn said. "He

just set a new speed record."

"Los Angeles to New York in eleven hours and thirty minutes," John said. "Think of it—three thousand miles in a half a day! I wish I could fly a plane that fast."

"But it's pretty dangerous, flying around like that," Uncle Ralph pointed out.

"It can be," John agreed. "At some races, the pilots crash. Sometimes they get hurt. Or killed. But it's part of flying, taking that risk. You never know what's going to happen."

"Let's not talk about crashes," Mr. Glenn said. "Think about the races."

"And they have stunt flying and parachute jumping, too," John said. "Hundreds of thousands of people will be there. This is going to be great!"

Around dusk, Mr. Glenn pulled into a campground just outside Cleveland. The four men set up their tents. Before going to bed, John lay out under the stars, studying the sky. "Someday," he said to himself. "I'll be up there someday."

The next morning, John and the others arrived early at the airport. Spectators were already filling the wooden stands that covered the field. John scrambled up to the highest bench. "I want to get as close to the planes as I can," he told his cousin.

They watched some of the stunt flyers. John enjoyed it for a while, then grew bored. "Come on," he said. "Let's start the race."

Finally, a loudspeaker crackled. "Ladies and gentlemen, we now come to today's featured event. Welcome to the Eighth Thompson Trophy Race, the world's premier aviation race."

"This is it," John said, nudging his cousin. "And there's Roscoe!" John nearly jumped out of his seat as he watched the famous pilot stride toward his plane.

"He flew more than two hundred eighty miles per hour to qualify for this race," John said. "Can you imagine traveling that fast?"

"Too bad he doesn't take passengers, huh?" Mr. Glenn said.

The announcer's voice once again boomed over the loudspeaker. "In this race, the pilots will fly thirty laps around a ten-mile course. Each pilot must circle the pylons that mark the course. The race will begin in just a few moments."

John watched Turner climb into his silver-colored plane. The other pilots were entering their planes, but Turner acted as if the rest of the world didn't exist. John was fascinated with the pilot's intense concentration with the flight ahead.

The roar of engines filled the field. The signal came, and the planes scrambled down the runways and into the air.

"Sounds like bees in a tin can," John shouted over the noise of the circling planes. The aircraft made tight turns around the fifty-foot-tall pylons, their wings dipping around the curves. On one part of the course, the planes thundered directly above the spectators. John felt the power of the engines vibrate in his stomach.

"Who's ahead?" Bob shouted.

100

"It looks like . . . yeah, it's Turner!" John yelled. "But Earl Ortman is right behind him."

Flying at close to three hundred miles per hour, Turner circled the course every few minutes. John bounced in his seat as the pilot extended his lead. John imagined himself in the cockpit of Turner's plane, banking through the corners and zooming down the straightaways.

"This is it," Mr. Glenn said. "Last lap."

Turner streaked across the finish line, winning his second Thompson Trophy. The huge crowd stood and applauded. No one clapped and stomped louder than John. "Way to go, Roscoe!" he cheered.

After about a minute, John sat down on again. His body felt limp, drained by the excitement of the race.

"Not a bad flight, eh, Bud?" Mr. Glenn asked.

"It was great!"

On the ride back to New Concord, John didn't talk much. Instead, he looked out the window, searching the sky for planes. Maybe they were headed for Cleveland. Maybe even farther away, like Chicago or New York. "I'm going to fly someday," John said. He barely said the words aloud. "Soon."

"Oh, yeah?" Bob said. "What do Uncle Herschel and Aunt Clara say about it?"

Mr. Glenn looked at the two boys in his rearview mirror. "We've heard about this idea," he said. "But I'm not so sure it's a done deal."

"But, Dad, you know it's what I want to do," John protested.

"I know," Mr. Glenn said." But *you* know how dangerous it can be. Why would you want to take that kind of risk for no reason?"

"I don't care about the risks. Besides, I won't be a racer, like Roscoe Turner. I'll fly passenger planes. One of those clippers that cross the ocean."

"We'll see," Mr. Glenn said, without much enthusiasm.

"You gotta learn how to fly first," Bob said. "How are you going to do that?"

"Lessons. I'll get the money somehow."

But John knew money was what held him back from his dream. With all his school activities, he didn't have much time to work. What he made during the summer barely paid for keeping the Cruiser running and going out with Annie. Mr. Glenn's business was doing better, but he couldn't afford to pay for lessons. John figured his father wouldn't pay for them even if he could afford it.

John sat back in his seat and sighed. Just one more year of school, he thought to himself. Then I have to find a way to fly.

Airborne at Last

John's senior year passed quickly, and in the fall of 1939 he entered Muskingum College. To save money, John lived at home. Annie was already at the school, studying music. Their relationship continued to grow, and they talked about marriage. At school, John decided to study chemistry. He also went out for the football team. But as his first year went on, John paid more attention to events on the other side of the Atlantic Ocean.

Germany was now ruled by Adolf Hitler, the brutal leader of the Nazi Party. Hitler and his Nazi followers had taken away the legal rights of Germany's Jewish citizens. Now Hitler wanted to rule most of Europe. On September 1, 1939, Germany invaded Poland. The invasion drew Great Britain and France into a war against Germany. The Second World War had begun.

By mid-1940, Germany controlled France and most of Western Europe. At the end of the summer, the Germans launched bombing raids on Great Britain. When John returned to school that fall, he read about the heroic flights of Great Britain's pilots in the Royal Air Force, or RAF.

"Did you see today's paper?" John asked his friend Carl Anker.

"You mean the baseball scores from last night?"

"Carl—I mean the war. The Battle of Britain! The British planes shot down sixty German bombers. Can't you imagine being in one of those RAF Spitfires, tangling with a Nazi plane?"

"Be careful what you wish for, John. America

could still get sucked into this war, you know. You could find yourself behind the controls of a fighter yet."

"I don't know, Carl," John said. "A lot of people around here want us to stay out. Look at Lindbergh—he says America shouldn't get involved."

John had read that his old hero, Charles "Lucky Lindy" Lindbergh, believed Americans had no business fighting in Europe. But as the war went on, John wondered how long the United States could stay neutral. Most people seemed to back the British. If the country did go to war, John knew he would do his part, just as his father had in 1918.

One day early in 1941, John and Carl headed for a class in the science building. They saw a group of students crowding around a bulletin board.

"What's up?" John asked the boy in front of him.

106

"It's some pilot training course."

John's face lit up. "Here? In New Concord?"

"Nah," the boy replied. "But not too far away."

"Does it cost much?"

"Get this," the boy said. "It's free—*if* you qualify. The federal government's paying for it."

John couldn't believe it. He politely nudged his way through the crowd so he could read the notice.

"What's it say?" Carl called to him from the rear.

"It's all true," John shouted back. "The government will pay for classes and flight lessons. If you pass the course, you get your pilot's license."

"Are you gonna do it?" Carl asked.

John smiled. "Are you kidding?"

That night at dinner, John squirmed in his chair, waiting to tell his parents the news. For years, the Glenns had always done the same thing at dinner. Everyone took a few minutes to describe what they had done that day. Jean had barely finished talking about her day at school when John burst out, "I'm going to be a pilot!"

Mr. and Mrs. Glenn looked at each other.

"Well," John said, "I have to apply first, and take classes, but I know I'll pass. I've never wanted anything more in my life."

"What's this all about?" Mr. Glenn finally asked.

John explained the program and how he could get his pilot's license. "And it won't cost us a cent," John said. "I've worried for so long about getting enough money for lessons, but now—"

"Bud," Mr. Glenn interrupted. "It's not money that I'm worried about."

"What do you mean, Dad?"

"I'm worried about you. I have to tell you, I'm not in favor of this."

"Why not?" John asked, his face twisted in pain.

"It's too dangerous."

Mrs. Glenn nodded. "They're always crashing in those planes."

"It's not too dangerous if you know what you're

doing," John asserted. "I'll learn how to do it right, and always be careful."

"John, I just get a sick feeling in my stomach when I think of you flying," Mr. Glenn said. "And if anything else happens in Europe, with the war . . ."

"Bud, let's not talk about this anymore right now," Mrs. Glenn said. "You just think about it."

"I've been thinking about it for years," John muttered. The Glenns finished their meal in silence.

John had one last hope for getting into the flying class. The man in charge of the program at Muskingum was Dr. Paul Martin. "Doc," as he was known, was a friend of the family. John convinced him to come to the house and speak to his parents.

"Herschel, Clara, I understand your concerns," Doc Martin said. "But look at the practical side. Aviation is a growing industry in this country. John will learn some skills that could lead to a good job."

"I never thought about that," Mr. Glenn admitted. "Still, it would be a pretty dangerous job."

"Every job has its dangers, Herschel. Some big pipe could drop on your head at a plumbing job. You can't worry about it. You accept the risks. Besides, John's a smart guy. You know that."

"Yes, Doc, we know that."

"I'd say he'll make an excellent pilot."

John watched his parents closely.

"Clara?" Mr. Glenn said.

Mrs. Glenn took her husband's hand. "Do you think it's all right?"

Mr. Glenn nodded.

"Go ahead, Bud," Mrs. Glenn said. "Just promise me this—you'll be the best pilot you can be."

John's application was accepted, and within a few weeks he was taking his first class. He learned how a plane flew, and all the forces that affected it during flight. The class work was interesting, but John couldn't wait for his first flight lesson. In

April, John and some of the other students drove to the airport in New Philadelphia, Ohio.

"It's just a grass strip," said John's friend Dane Handschy.

"And check out that crate," another student said, pointing to the training plane. "It's so puny."

"It's a Taylorcraft," John said, walking over to the plane. "And it looks just fine to me."

A tall, slender man joined the students. He was barely older than John. "All right guys, let's get started," the man said. "My name is Wally Spotts, and I'm going to teach you how to fly—I hope. I'll be up there with you the first few times, so if you mess up, we're both going to pay for it."

The other students chuckled. John just kept admiring the plane.

"The first few times out," Wally went on, "we're going to take it easy. You'll learn how to taxi on the ground, then fly level, with no turns. After a few weeks we'll get you into some more complicated things."

Two or three days a week, John and the other

students traveled to New Philadelphia for their flight lessons. Each time he took control of the plane, a jolt of energy surged through John's body. He tried to explain it to Annie. "It's like all my senses are so sharp. I can see more clearly, hear the softest noise. And my mind is so focused. All I can think about is the plane, and doing what I'm supposed to do."

"So you think y-y-you'll be a good p-p-pilot?" Annie asked.

"I don't want to brag . . . but, yeah, I do. I think I can be really good. It's like I was meant to fly."

In May, John made his first solo flight. He took off and landed smoothly. For the next few weeks, Wally taught him more difficult turns, and John practiced landing under all different conditions. In late June, John took his final test for his pilot's license. He scored a ninety-six.

"There's one more thing you need," Wally told him. "My recommendation."

John paced a bit in front of his instructor. "And?"

"And I think you'll do fine," Wally said. "I gave

the recommendation already. John, you were one of the best pilots here."

Just a few days before his twentieth birthday, John Glenn was a licensed pilot.

In the fall of 1941, John started his third year at Muskingum. The news from overseas took more of his interest. The Germans now controlled more of Europe and part of North Africa. They had also launched a surprise attack against the Soviet Union. John tried to stay focused on his classes and on Annie. But one day in December, the war finally came to America.

On the seventh, Annie was giving an organ recital at the school. Driving over to the concert, John turned on the radio.

"We have a news bulletin," the radio announcer said. "Japanese planes have just attacked the U.S. naval base at Pearl Harbor, Hawaii. The damage seems to be heavy, with many deaths and injuries. We will give you updates as more information becomes available."

"A surprise attack!" John said out loud. "By the Japanese!" Tensions between Japan and the United States had been growing. Japan was friendly with Nazi Germany. And Japan had been taking over neighboring countries in Asia. But few Americans expected an attack like this.

John thought about the news report all through the concert. When it ended, he rushed over to Annie to tell her the news. "You know what this means?" John asked her.

"W-w-war," she said sadly. "What are y-y-you going to do?"

"I have to enlist," John said. "I have to fly for my country."

A few days later, John signed up for the U.S. Army Air Corps.

Months passed, and John never received his orders to report to the army. He decided to enlist again, this time with the U.S. Navy. The navy quickly accepted him into its pilot program. After a tearful good-bye with Annie and his family,

John headed to Iowa City, Iowa, for basic training. For three months, John drilled and took classes. When this training ended, he headed to Kansas for navy flight school.

In Kansas, John flew a Stearman biplane. This craft was bigger and more powerful that the plane he had first trained on. John learned the moves he would need in a midair battle—a dogfight. He took the Stearman through big loops, or rolled it in a tight spiral.

John's training continued in Texas. By now, he had a new friend, a red-haired Texan named Tom Miller. They shared a love of flying and soon became the two top pilots in their class.

One day, John and Tom passed a notice outside their barracks.

"Hey, Miller, Glenn," another pilot called. "You two are such hotshots. Check this out."

John read the bulletin. "It says pilots with good enough grades can join the marines. There's a guy coming tonight to talk about it."

"Want to go?" Tom asked.

"Sure. Though I can't say I ever thought about the marines."

That night, a group of pilots filled a small hall. At the front, a young marine captain talked about the fighting at Guadalcanal. Marines were winning the battle on this small Pacific island.

"And you may not know it," the captain said, "but our pilots are playing a big part in these battles. The marines are the toughest soldiers around. If you want to be the best, you should be flying for the marines."

The captain paused and looked around the room. "But to tell you the truth, I don't think any of you are good enough to be one of us."

"Who does he think he is?" John whispered to Tom. "He can't tell me I'm not good enough."

"He's just saying that," Tom said. "He wasn't talking to *you*."

"Well, I'm not going to take that," John said. "I'll show him."

116

Before the meeting ended, John filled out a form. He was going to prove he was good enough to fly for the marines.

Off to War

Within months, John was a second lieutenant in the United States Marines. He proudly wore his new uniform on April 6, 1943, when he and Annie finally married. After a short honeymoon, the couple left for John's next stop, the marine aviation base at Cherry Point, North Carolina. From there, the Glenns went on to El Centro, California. In the hot desert, John learned how to fly fighter planes.

In September, John's squadron received their planes: the F4U Corsairs. John and Tom Miller

inspected their new aircraft.

"They say she's tough to land," Tom said.

"We'll get the hang of it," said John.

"And look at that canopy." Tom inspected the domed, glass roof that covered the pilots as they flew. The canopy on the Corsair was crisscrossed with metal bars. "It looks like a birdcage."

"But check out this engine," John said. "Two thousand horsepower. That's more than any other fighter. We'll be cruising at over four hundred miles per hour in this thing!"

A month later, a new model of the Corsair arrived at El Centro. With it came a special instructor—Charles Lindbergh. The plane's manufacturer had asked the famous pilot to explain the improvements on the Corsair.

"Can you believe it," John bubbled to Tom. "Charles Lindbergh is here. My boyhood hero. Look, there he is on the airfield. Let's go meet him."

"Sure," Tom said. "I'm sure he'll be thrilled to meet that other famous pilot, John Glenn."

The two pilots approached the plane that Lindbergh was examining. After a minute, a general introduced them to the aviation hero.

"Mr. Lindbergh, this is such an honor," John said. "I learned all about you and the *Spirit of St. Louis* when I was first old enough to read."

"Well, thank you—"

"And I hung models of your plane from my ceiling," John went on.

"That's—"

"And I've always been inspired by you and your heroic flight."

"Thank you, Lieutenant Glenn," Lindbergh finally said. "Maybe you have your own heroics ahead of you. Fly well, Lieutenant."

"Thank you, sir," John said.

"'Did you hear that?" John said to Tom as they walked away. "'Fly well,'" John repeated. "'Fly well.'"

John and his squadron spent the next few months training on the Corsair. Finally, they received orders to head into battle. John said good-bye to Annie, then set sail for Hawaii. From there, the squadron went on to Midway. This tiny island was farther west in the Pacific Ocean. In June 1942, the waters off Midway had been the setting of a huge battle between Japanese and American forces. U.S. planes destroyed four Japanese aircraft carriers. The Americans lost just one. Since then, Midway had become a base for the U.S. submarine fleet. For John, Midway was the last stop before his first combat duty.

On June 28, 1944, John left Midway for the Marshall Islands. On the voyage to the Marshalls, John relaxed with his friends. Besides Tom, John now spent time with Monty Goodman. They had become friendly in California. Monty was a fun-loving guy. He entertained the pilots with imitations of Frank Sinatra, the most popular singer of the day. John and his friends also played volley-ball on the ship. When he had free time, John read or wrote long letters to Annie.

Within a week, the squadron reached Majuro Harbor, in the Marshall Islands. The Marshalls are a series of tiny islands that stretch out for more than two thousand miles. Some of the islands are no more than strips of coral called atolls. U.S. forces had captured some of the larger Marshall Islands in February 1944. The Japanese still controlled some nearby atolls. John and the other pilots were to make sure the Japanese did not build up their defenses on those atolls.

A week went by before John received orders for his first combat flight.

"Glenn, have your division ready," said Major Pete Haines. "We're hitting Maloelap Atoll."

"Yes, sir," John said.

"Are you prepared for this? No nerves?"

John smiled. "No, sir, no nerves. We're ready. It's why we've been training so hard all these months."

"You know, Glenn," the major continued, "some of the other officers are jealous of you."

"Sir?" John was slightly puzzled.

"Leading a division of planes is an honor for someone your age. A sign of my trust in you."

"Yes, sir," John said. "I appreciate it, sir."

"Here's your chance to really earn it."

The other pilots in John's division were Tom, Monty, and Ed Powers. John called them together and explained the mission.

"We're going in over Maloelap, about one hundred ten miles north of here. We're flying ahead of the bombers. We come down and knock out the antiaircraft guns. Or at least keep them busy while the bombers do their work. Then we get the heck out of there. Any questions?"

"Do you have any requests?" Monty asked.

"Huh?"

"Requests. What Sinatra song should I sing while we're going in?"

John laughed. He liked the way Monty always kept his sense of humor. "No songs. No radio contact at all. The idea is to surprise the enemy, not serenade them. You can sing your heart out on the way back."

Soon John's planes and the other division in his flight group were ready for takeoff. Behind them flew the dive-bombers. As the planes neared the target, John looked next to him. He saw Monty grinning in his cockpit. John gave a signal, and the planes in his division dived down toward the atoll.

John flew straight down at the Japanese guns. He squeezed the trigger on his controls. Under the wings, six cannons roared to life. John saw his fire ripping through the target below.

"So far so good," John said to himself. The orange glow of Japanese gunfire streaked by the Corsair, but none hit their target. John flew low over the treetops, then pulled the plane up into the sky. As he flew higher, he saw black smoke behind him. The dive-bombers had hit their targets, too.

John flew to eight thousand feet, where he was supposed to meet with the rest of the planes. From the two divisions, only seven planes came out of the clouds.

"Where's Monty?" John called into his radio. "Red two, are you aboard? Red two—where are you?"

John and the other pilots flew back toward the atoll. They tried to guess where Monty might have flown after firing his guns.

"Over there," someone radioed. "To the left."

John saw a long slick of oil on the ocean's surface. It was a sure sign that Monty's plane had gone down.

"I think I see something yellow," another pilot radioed.

"It's the dye from his life jacket," John said. All the pilots wore life jackets. The jackets released a dye that made it easier for search planes to spot pilots in the water.

"Keep looking!" John ordered.

The Corsairs searched the area for two hours.

"I'm getting low on fuel," Tom Miller finally radioed. "Have to turn back."

John looked at his own fuel gauge. He was almost on empty, too. No one had seen Monty. But now they had no choice but to go back to Majuro.

Back at the base, Major Haines told the other

pilots the bad news. "Lieutenant Goodman is missing in action," the major said. "And presumed dead."

John had known that Monty was not coming back. The major's words made it too real. At his bunk, John got down on his knees and cried for his friend. "This is what war's really about," he said to himself. "It's not just flying high and being a hero. People—friends, sons, fathers—die."

John decided to write a letter to Monty's parents in Pennsylvania. He explained what a good friend Monty had been to him. He told the Goodmans what a fine pilot Marty was.

"He always hung in there, no matter what," John carefully wrote. "He meant a lot to all of us. And I want you to know this, Mr. and Mrs. Goodman. From now on, we're all fighting for Monty. It's our way of remembering him."

New missions came almost every day. Sometimes John flew twice a day. Usually he dropped bombs from his Corsair. At times, John and the other pilots met heavy enemy fire. But each time out, John returned safely to Majuro.

One day Major Haines came over to talk with John. "You seem to like this flying business," the major said.

"Yes, sir," John replied. "I've never felt happier then when I'm in my Corsair. It's like I don't even have to think about flying anymore. I just do it. It's like breathing."

"Dangerous breathing," Major Haines added.

John shrugged. "Yes, sir, I know. But it doesn't matter, when I'm up there."

"John, we could use men like you in the marines after the war. You should consider signing up for a military career."

"I'd never thought about that before, Major."

"I hope you will now. You can apply, then you can always change your mind later on."

"I think I will, sir," John said slowly. "Thank you."

Through the rest of 1944, John and his

squadron flew out of different islands in the Marshalls. On one run, John led the strike against the Japanese target. His Corsair held a two thousand–pound bomb. He swooped over the target, dropped his bomb, then pulled up into the sky. A moment later, the plane shook with a tremendous force.

"I think I've been hit," John radioed.

"What's the damage?" Tom responded from his plane.

John looked out the canopy. He saw a huge chunk of metal missing from his wing.

"It's on the wing," he said. "But the controls seem okay."

"I see it now," Tom said. "Looks like the hit is close to the oil cooler."

"Uh-oh. That's not good."

If the engine oil overheated or leaked out, the engine would stop working. If that happened, John knew he would have to bail out. He had his parachute and a life jacket. But the waters below were filled with sharks. John prayed the engine would hold out.

"Think you'll make it?" Tom asked.

"If the cooler's okay, I'll be fine," John said. "Cross your fingers."

John's luck held out. The engine and the cooler weren't damaged, and the Corsair made it back to the base.

Soon after that close call, John flew his last mission. Then he wrote one last letter to Annie. "It's hard to believe I've been on combat duty for a year. I've flown fifty-nine missions and been hit by antiaircraft fire five times. I've dropped more bombs than I can count. And I've been lucky enough to win some medals. But none of that is important now. I'm finally coming home to you."

Korea

"I've got to get out of here!"

"J-John, please. You'll w-w-wake Lyn. She's n-napping."

John paced around the small apartment. It was October 1952. He and Annie had a family now: Dave was almost seven, and Lyn was five. The Glenns lived on a base at Quantico, Virginia.

"I didn't stay in the marines for this," John said, lowering his voice. "Taking classes, teaching classes. I'm never in a plane. I want to fly."

"Did y-y-ou s-s-send another l-letter?" Annie asked.

John nodded. "I'm still waiting to hear back. But with my luck, I'll get the same reply: 'Request denied.' I can't believe they can't use a pilot with my skills over in Korea."

"So, y-y-you think you can w-w-win this war?" Annie teased.

"That's not what I meant," John said. "But I can do my part."

Since July 1950, the United States had been fighting in Korea. It was the first major combat of the Cold War. When World War II ended, America and the Soviet Union began a struggle for influence around the world. The Soviet Union promoted a political system called communism. Americans opposed communism because it limited individual freedom. The United States was trying to stop the spread of communism and support democratic countries.

In Asia, the Communist government of North Korea attacked South Korea. The South Koreans favored democracy. The North Koreans received support from the Soviet

132

Union and the Communist government of China. Now the Americans were fighting to help the South Koreans.

A few days later, John finally got his wish. He received orders to go to South Korea. Once again, he said good-bye to Annie and left to serve his country.

In February 1953, John arrived at P'ohang. The winter wind there seemed to rip through his body. Around the base, John saw villages destroyed by the war. After almost three years of fighting, neither side was close to a victory.

Some things had changed since John last saw combat. Now the marines flew jet planes. These aircraft were faster and easier to maneuver than the old Corsairs. John's squadron flew F9F Panthers. They carried bombs and packed powerful cannons. Just as he had in the Marshall Islands, John flew dive-bombing runs at enemy targets.

Soon after he arrived in Korea, John received a visit from Tom Miller. Tom had already been flying missions in the war. "Let me give you some advice, John," he said. "The North Koreans aren't like the Japanese. They have lots more antiaircraft guns and they know how to use them. When you're on a bombing run, drop your load and get out. If you try to knock out a gun site, you're asking for trouble. For every gun you see, there's three or four hidden out of sight."

"Okay, Tom," John said. "Thanks for the tip."

John remembered Tom's advice every time he flew. But on one mission, John couldn't resist going for an antiaircraft site. As John went in to drop his bomb, he saw the flash of guns off to his right.

I'll be back for you later, John thought to himself. He finished his dive and flew low along the treetops. Then he circled back to where he saw the antiaircraft fire. With his four cannons flashing, John took out the gun site.

"No more Panthers for you," John said with satisfaction. He pulled up the plane to head back to the base. Suddenly, he felt the tail shake violently, and the plane's nose began to dip. "What the—I'm hit!"

John reacted without thinking to pull the plane back up. Flying at close to five hundred miles per hour, the Panther almost grazed a hilltop. More gunfire burst around the jet.

"Come on, baby," John said. "Get me out of this!"

John radioed to the base. "I've been bounced." He used the pilot's slang for "attacked." "I took some kind of hit in the tail."

When he landed, John examined the plane. A huge section of the tail had been blown away.

"Ooh man," said Woody Woodbury, one of the other pilots. "You could throw a pony through that hole."

"I can't even count the other hits," John said. "There must be hundreds of them."

"Glenn, you must have a magnet in your butt," Woody joked. "You just draw the bullets right to you."

A few days later, John saw Tom Miller again.

He told Tom what had happened during the mission. "I thought I was going to dig a crater in the side of that hill," John said, "and never come back out. From now on, I'll take your advice—no turning back."

In just a few months, John flew sixty-three missions. He took antiaircraft fire again, and he saw other pilots have close calls with death. Still, John was ready for another risk—flying a jet fighter.

"One-on-one," John said to Tom. "Just you and another pilot dogging it out thousands of feet in the air."

"No dogfights for me," Tom said. "You've got to have some pretty tough nerves for that. And those Soviet MiGs are good planes."

Pilots from the Soviet Union flew the MiG-15 jets for North Korea. The Soviets attacked the U.S. planes on their bombing runs.

"But the Sabre is even better," John insisted.

The F86-Sabre was the top U.S. fighter jet.

The Sabre and the MiG were similar. Both could fly faster than the speed of sound—about 670 miles per hour. The MiG flew a little higher than the Sabre, but the U.S. jet could fly farther. The Sabre also turned faster in flight.

"Besides," John said, "the pilot's just as important as the plane. I know I could shoot down my share of MiGs."

The marines didn't fly the Sabre. The plane was an air force jet. John applied for a special program that let marine pilots fly for the air force. He was accepted, and soon he was making his first mission in the Sabre. But after a few times out, he started to grow bored. Each time he searched the sky for MiGs but saw nothing. "Where the heck are they?" John wondered. "At this rate I'll never be an ace." A pilot who shot down five MiGs in dogfights earned the title "ace."

Major Giraudo, John's commander, laughed. "What's the matter John, you afraid the war will be over before you get an MiG?"

"It could," John said. "I didn't come over here

to fly pleasure trips. I want to see some action."

For days, John complained about not spotting any Soviet planes. One morning, he walked out to his Sabre and saw a slogan painted on its side. The huge letters said, "MiG Mad Marine."

"Very funny," John said to the other pilots. He thought about painting over the new nickname, but decided to keep it. "Maybe it'll bring me luck."

A few weeks later, in mid-July, John was still looking for his first MiG "kill." On patrol at 23,000 feet, he finally spotted one.

"I'm going after him," John radioed to the other Sabres nearby. He followed the MiG into a cloud but lost sight of the enemy jet. Coming out of the cloud, John saw a second MiG. He began to chase it. The two planes dropped to about two thousand feet. The Soviet plane headed for nearby China. Forty miles over the Chinese border, the MiG suddenly slowed down. John's Sabre almost rammed the plane in the rear.

What's he up to? John thought. He looked

down. An airfield! The MiG was trying to return to its base.

"Not so fast, bud," John said. He fired his machine guns. Bullets ripped through the MiG's body and wings, and flames erupted from the plane.

"All right!" John shouted. "That's a kill!" He watched the MiG crash to the earth. By now, the Sabre was only fifty feet off the ground. John flew through a cloud of black smoke from the burning MiG. When he looked up, he saw the control tower of the airfield directly in front of him. John blasted again with his guns, then pulled up to head back to base.

When John landed, the flight crew gathered around his plane.

"Check out that black nose," one of the crewmen said. "Someone's been letting those Soviets have it real good." After firing, the Sabre's machine guns left a telltale black powder on the front of the plane.

John sat in his cockpit and smiled.

"Gentlemen, there is one less MiG over the skies of South Korea." The crew cheered. "That's number one, with more to come."

John kept his word. A few days later, just after his thirty-second birthday, he scored another kill. This one was not so easy. The MiG pilot didn't turn and run. Instead, he banked and circled so he could fire at John's plane. John made a hard turn, and the bullets missed. Another Sabre pilot then hit the MiG with two bursts from his guns. Soon, John came across six more Soviet jets. They weren't so eager for combat and flew off. John trailed the last one and fired. The MiG burst into flames and went down. Three days later, John added a third kill.

"Just two more to go," John said to Sam Young, another pilot. "Then you can call me 'Ace' Glenn."

"I wouldn't count on it, John," said Sam. "Didn't you hear the news?"

"What do you mean?"

"The peace talks," Sam explained. "They

finally reached an agreement. The war's over."

John looked surprised. Then he smiled. "I guess that's the only good reason for my not getting those other two MiGs. Thank God it's over."

The Korean War ended on July 27, 1953. John stayed in South Korea through the end of the year. He wrote to Lyn and David, explaining that he wouldn't be home for the holidays. Then John wrote another letter. He already had plans for what he wanted to do when he returned to America.

New Tests

Flying at 44,000 feet, John took the FJ-3 Fury over the Atlantic Ocean. John had gotten the new job he wanted. He now flew as a test pilot for the U.S. Navy. America was still waging the Cold War with the Soviet Union. The navy needed the best planes possible for any future combat. Test pilots such as John made sure the planes worked correctly. They also took the risks if a new plane didn't fly right.

On this flight, John was testing the Fury's cannons. He flew over the test area and squeezed the trigger. The cannons roared into the empty sky.

"It's going well," John said to himself. "Everything seems to be—"

John heard a "pop." He looked around the cockpit. He noticed the seal of the canopy had broken. Air from outside the plane began to rush in. At 44,000 feet, the air is "thin"—it doesn't have enough oxygen in it for a person to breathe. With the canopy sealed tight, the air inside the plane was fine. But now, the air inside the plane was turning deadly.

John knew what to do. He switched on a backup supply of oxygen. "That should do it," he said.

But within a few seconds, John knew something was still wrong. Everything looked strange. Black splotches seemed to float in front of him.

"Still not right," John said. The black spots meant his brain wasn't getting enough oxygen. He knew that within a few seconds, he would black out. The Fury would plummet out of control to Earth, some eight miles below. Gotta go for the apple, John thought.

The "apple" was a green, wooden ball attached to a cord. By pulling on the cord, John would start his last emergency supply of oxygen. The cord was connected to a small bottle of oxygen in his parachute pack.

The circles of black grew bigger in front of John's eyes. As he struggled for air, he could feel a growing pressure on his lungs. It was as if a huge hand were crushing his body. John grabbed the apple. With all his strength, he pulled. A second later, he took a deep breath. Oxygen filled his lungs. Slowly, his eyes began to clear. He was all right.

"Man," John said, sighing. "Never a dull moment when you're a test pilot."

John flew out of the Naval Air Test Center at Patuxent River, Maryland. From August 1954 to November 1956, he flew the Fury and other top navy fighter jets. One of his favorites was the F8U Crusader. The plane held a national aviation speed record of 1,015 miles per hour. Late in 1956, John had an idea for how he could test the Crusader's limits, and show the country how good the navy planes were.

"Listen to this," John said to Bill Russell, another test pilot. "Some air force jet holds the record for fastest flight across America, right?"

"Yeah," Bill said. "Something like three hours and fifty minutes."

"Three forty-five," John corrected. "Well, I think I can top that in the Crusader. I'm going to ask Washington if I can fly a test mission across the country."

"A test mission?" Bill asked.

"Sure. We still don't know for sure how the plane handles at high altitudes, going at top speed for long distance. I can take the Crusader up for the test—and go for the speed record."

"Sounds good," Bill said. "But you know the navy. It could take months to get an okay—*if* you get one."

"I know," John said. "That's why I'm starting

tomorrow. I want to do this as soon as I can."

John went to work, doing research and talking to engineers. He figured he would have to refuel three times during the flight. Tanker planes would meet him along the route. The tankers flew close to fighter planes and refueled them using long fuel lines. The refueling operation would slow John down, but he still thought he and the Crusader could beat the speed record.

Three times John discussed his plan with top Navy officials. Three times they turned him down. Finally, in mid-1957, he got the word— the cross-country flight was a go. But when he heard the news, John was not completely happy. "They messed around with my plans," he said to Annie. "I have to use slower tanker planes than I had hoped. And I won't be flying alone."

"Who else is g-g-oing?" Annie asked.

"Some pilot named Charlie Demmler. He'll be in another Crusader. But I did come up with a great name for the flight."

"Yes?"

John made a fast, zooming motion with his hand. "Project Bullet."

At 6:04 A.M. on July 16, 1957, John took off from a naval base in California. A half hour later, Charlie Demmler took off in his Crusader. Project Bullet was underway. John's destination was New York. Reporters and TV crews were already waiting there, hoping John would break the speed record.

John took his jet up to fifty thousand feet and quickly hit a speed of more than one thousand miles per hour. Over New Mexico, he prepared for his first midair refueling. He slowed the Crusader and settled down to 25,000 feet.

"Fill 'er up," John joked with the tanker pilot.

"Check the oil too?" the pilot radioed back.

"Nah, that's okay. I'm in kind of a hurry."

After a few minutes, John was back to his cruising altitude and roaring along at top speed. The second fueling came over Kansas. This one also went smoothly. By now, John had heard that

Charlie Demmler and the second Crusader had been forced to land. If John didn't set the speed record, no one would.

The last refueling came over Indiana. John dropped down and searched the sky. "Where's that tanker?" he wondered. Suddenly, his radio crackled.

"Primary tanker is out of range," the voice said. "This is your backup. We've got you in sight and will be there shortly."

"Roger," John said with a trace of disappointment. The second tanker could not pump fuel as fast. The delay would cost him precious seconds. Then, during the refueling, the tanker pulled away too early. John was now short of fuel. But he couldn't worry about that now. He quickly pushed the Crusader back over one thousand miles per hour. His flight path took him over his hometown of New Concord. He knew that down below, his parents and old friends were cheering him on.

As John approached New York, he checked

his gas gauge. "Barely enough," he said. He breathed a sigh of relief as he spotted the airport below. He flew by the control tower, where the officials were timing his flight, then circled in for a landing. Annie and the kids ran over to greet the plane. So did the reporters who snapped his picture and shouted questions. First John had his own question. "What's the time?" he asked

"Three hours, twenty-three minutes, and eight point four seconds," someone shouted. "You beat the old record by twenty-one minutes!" The crowd cheered.

John's record-setting flight earned him national attention, as he soon appeared on television. He also won his fifth Distinguished Flying Cross, a medal for pilots. But just a few months after Project Bullet, Americans were no longer talking about Glenn and his plane. The whole world's attention turned even higher into the sky.

On October 4, 1957, the Soviet Union launched the first satellite into orbit around Earth. The satellite was called *Sputnik*—Russian for "companion." This steel orb was barely bigger than a basketball and weighed 184 pounds. It circled the planet one time every ninety-six minutes.

During the Cold War, the Soviet Union and the United States competed to have the best weapons. Now the two sides were about to begin a competition in space. This struggle to develop new technologies for space travel was soon called "the space race." John hoped he could help his country win this race.

In January 1958, the United States launched its own satellite. The government was also preparing to build larger spacecraft that would carry pilots. A new agency took over the plans for space flight. It was called the National Space and Aeronautics Administration (NASA). The agency called the pilots for its spacecraft "astronauts." NASA decided to take the first astronauts from experienced military pilots. John immediately made plans to apply.

"Aren't you g-g-getting too old f-f-for this?" Annie wondered.

"I'm thirty-seven now," John replied. "NASA's limit is thirty-nine."

"And wh-what about your weight?"

John looked at his body. He *had* gained a few pounds since his days in Korea. "Well, I guess I'll need to lose about thirty pounds. But I can do it."

"Tell me a-g-gain exactly what you'll b-b-be doing," Annie said.

"The astronauts will circle Earth."

"You'll f-f-fly into space."

"Not fly," John explained. "I'll be launched on a rocket—*if* I'm chosen."

Annie shook her head. "It sounds d-d-dangerous."

"Annie, everything I've done in my life has been dangerous. We both accept that. And this is something I know I can do well. It's something no one has ever done before. Imagine being one hundred miles above Earth and looking down."

Annie shook her head. "I can't. It's too s-s-scary."

"Not for me. It's like a dream, to be that high.

Except it will all be real. The Soviets are going to try to do the same thing, but we have to do it first. And I want to play my part."

"Y-you want me to say it's all r-r-right," Annie said.

"Only if it *is* all right," John said.

Annie smiled and hugged her husband. "It's all right."

The NASA mission to put a human in space was called Project Mercury. More than eighty pilots volunteered. The government quickly reduced that number to thirty-two. Only seven would be chosen for Project Mercury. John was still on the list. He took a number of physical and mental tests. No one knew how humans would react to space travel, but NASA wanted astronauts who were in good shape and could handle pressure. When the testing ended, all John could do was wait.

On April 6, 1959, John got a call.

"Major Glenn," the voice said. "This is Charles Donlan at NASA."

"Good afternoon, sir," said John. He held his breath. This was it—either he was in or out.

"You did well on all the tests. Are you still interested in Project Mercury?"

"Yes, sir," John almost shouted into the phone.

"Good. Congratulations—you're now an astronaut."

Into Space

A few days later, John and the six other Mercury astronauts gathered at Langley Air Force Base in Virginia. With John were Wally Schirra, Deke Slayton, Gus Grissom, Alan Shepard, Gordon Cooper, and Scott Carpenter.

Before leaving for Langley, John had made an important decision. Annie and the kids would stay at their new home in Arlington, Virginia. John would go to the base alone.

"I want Lyn and David to stay at their own

schools," he told Annie. "And I need to focus on my training. Are you all right with that?"

Annie smiled. "If it's wh-what you need to d-d-do, then you know it's all r-r-ight with me."

"It's what I need to do."

The next day, the astronauts met reporters for the first time. John seemed the most comfortable in front of the cameras and microphones. As the oldest astronaut, he took a role as spokesman for the group.

"Tell us, Colonel Glenn," one reporter said. "Why did you volunteer for the Mercury Project?"

"I got into this program because it probably would be the nearest to heaven I would ever get, and I wanted to make the most of it." John smiled as the audience laughed. "No, seriously," he continued, "I think all seven of us up here know we have special talents. Every one of us would feel guilty if we didn't make the fullest use of those talents, for our country, for the whole world."

John worked hard to make sure he was in the best physical shape of his life. He ran for hours along the beach. He stretched his mind, as well, studying the new information he needed to fly a spacecraft. The training also included many hours of experiencing the forces of gravity he would feel in space.

Gravity is the force of nature that makes thrown objects fall to the ground. Gravity also keeps objects—such as people—on the ground. One "G" (or gravity) force is equal to the pressure a human feels on Earth. In space, humans feel zero gravity—they float. On a spacecraft, astronauts feel increased gravity of eight G's or more. At that force, a person can black out. Spacesuits would help John and the other astronauts function in space.

During their G force tests, special machines swung small capsules with the astronauts inside. The gravity force sometimes reached sixteen G's. After one test, John staggered out of the capsule.

"Boy, that is something I don't want to do every day," he said.

"Just a few times in space, right?" one of the technicians asked.

"That's right," John replied.

"You planning on getting up there first?" someone else asked.

"I think I've got a pretty good shot."

John believed he was talented enough to be the first person in space. But over time, the relationship among the astronauts worked against him. To the outside world, the seven astronauts were a team. But as the men lived and trained together, they didn't always get along.

John was convinced the astronauts had a special responsibility.

"We're public figures," he told the others. "The newspapers and TV stations watch everything we do. People expect a lot from us. We have to be on our best behavior at all times."

Not everyone agreed with John. Some of the astronauts liked to go out and have fun when they weren't training. They told John to mind his own business. He was not the most popular member of the "team."

Toward the end of 1960, NASA official Bob Gilruth held a meeting with the seven astronauts. "It's time for us to pick the astronaut for the first Mercury flight," said Gilruth. "We want you to help us out. We're going to take a peer vote."

John's heart sank. In a peer vote, each person picks one of the others in a group as the best person for a particular job. No one can vote for himself. John knew he wouldn't win. The other astronauts didn't like him enough to choose him for such a great honor. On his slip of paper he wrote, "Scott Carpenter." Then he waited to learn which of the other six would be the first astronaut in space.

A few weeks later, NASA made a public announcement. Either John, Alan Shepard, or Gus Grissom would make the first U.S. space flight. Privately, NASA told the men that

Shepard was the first choice. John tried to hide his disappointment.

As Shepard prepared for his flight, the Soviet Union once again leaped ahead in the space race. On April 12, 1961, Soviets cosmonaut Yuri Gagarin circled Earth on a space flight that lasted 108 minutes. The Mercury Program was not going to put the first human into space. Shepard's mission was also not as advanced as Garagin's flight. Shepard's was a suborbital flight. His craft would not fly high enough to orbit Earth. He would just shoot up into space and return a few minutes later. Shepard finally flew on May 5, but his mission seemed less important after Gagarin's historic flight.

The Americans had planned to make at least two more suborbital flights. Now NASA felt pressure to match the Soviets. After Gus Grissom flew the next suborbital flight, NASA was ready to fly an orbital mission. It was John's turn to fly—and hopefully make history for his country.

"This waiting is killing me!" John tapped his fist against his thigh.

"What can you do, John?" asked Scott Carpenter. "It's out of your hands."

John paced around the astronaut's quarters at Cape Canaveral, Florida. "The Cape" was the launch site for the Mercury missions.

"I'll go check on the capsule while you get ready," Carpenter said. "Just hope that the eleventh time is the charm."

Ten times before, NASA had picked out a date for his flight. Ten times John had been ready to go. And ten times NASA eventually said no. Bad weather or equipment problems always forced a delay. John once spent six hours crammed inside his spacecraft, called *Friendship 7*, before NASA cancelled the flight. Now it was February 20, 1962. John hoped this would finally be the day he went into space.

After breakfast, John slipped on his silver space suit. Driving over to the launch pad, John saw the sixty-five-foot Atlas rocket that would boost him and *Friendship 7* into orbit. For years, the U.S. rocket program had faced many problems. Some rockets, including one Atlas, had blown up just a few feet after liftoff. John tried not to think about everything that could go wrong with the flight.

Once he was strapped into the capsule, John heard Carpenter's voice over the radio.

"We have a mystery caller on the line. Want to take the call?"

"Go ahead," John said.

"H-hello, John." Annie's voice filled John's helmet.

"How are you and the kids doing?" he asked.

"We're f-f-fine. How are *you?*"

"Strapped in and ready to go. Don't worry about a thing. Remember, it's just like I'm going down to the corner for a pack of gum."

"Pr-pr-pretty far corner," Annie tried to joke. "D-don't take long."

When the conversation ended, John got ready in his seat. At 9:47 A.M., two huge rocket engines roared to life beneath him. The Atlas slowly lifted off the pad.

"We're off!" John said.

The rocket shuddered as it flew upward. This is it, John thought. If she's gonna blow, it's going to be now. The rocket hurtled on. After a few minutes, the *Friendship 7* capsule broke away from the rocket and entered orbit around Earth. John was traveling at 17,500 miles per hour.

"Zero G and I feel fine," John radioed in. He looked out his spacecraft's tiny window. He saw the Atlantic Ocean and the west coast of Africa. "You guys are missing a great view!"

Through the flight, instruments measured John's blood pressure. He performed some experiments, such as exercising, and took pictures. Everything was going fine.

"*Friendship 7,*" said a voice on the radio, "keep your landing bag switch in the off position."

"It is off," John said. "Is there a problem?"

"No problem. Just checking."

The landing bag was supposed to help John land safely when he returned to Earth. The craft would land in the ocean, and the bag would soften the crash. But if the bag had somehow come out while he was in space—John knew that could be trouble. A problem with the bag could mean there was a problem with the heat shield. The two pieces were located near each other on the bottom of the craft. The shield was designed to keep the spacecraft cool when it sped back toward Earth. But if NASA wasn't worried, neither was John.

Friendship 7 continued to orbit Earth. In just a few hours, he saw three different sunsets over the planet. John knew he was experiencing something rare and beautiful.

"*Friendship 7,* we're getting a signal that your landing bag has opened. We think it's a mistake, but we need to make sure."

Now John sensed something was wrong. "What should I do?" he asked.

"Put the landing bag switch in the 'auto' position and see if you turn on the light."

"But if the bag *isn't* out—"

"Roger, *Friendship 7.* If it's not out now,

flipping the switch might set it off."

And setting it off might create a problem with the heat shield, John knew. When he returned to Earth, the entire capsule could burn like tissue paper in a campfire.

"Ready to go?" the radio voice asked.

"Roger." John flipped the switch. The light did not come on. He quickly switched it back. "No light," he reported.

"Roger. We'll go ahead, and the reentry will be normal."

But everything was not yet normal. Mission control still received a signal that something was wrong with the landing bag. John knew he still faced a risk on reentry. As he prepared to come down, John imagined the heat he would feel if the shield failed. The temperature would hit 9,500 degrees Fahrenheit—almost as hot as the surface of the sun.

Mission control kept sending him commands. Suddenly, the radio cut off. This was normal during reentry. John actually enjoyed the silence.

Looking out the window, he saw an orange glow deepen all around the capsule. Flaming pieces of metal ripped past. "I don't know what that was," John said to himself. "Maybe I don't want to know."

All he could do was wait and see if the capsule survived the heat. John watched the controls. He kept one eye on the window. The orange glow was fading. He'd made it!

" . . . how do you read?" John recognized Alan Shepard's voice. The radio was working again.

"Loud and clear," John said. "Do you hear me?"

"Roger. How are you doing, *Friendship 7*?"

"Pretty good. But that was some fireball up there!"

As the spacecraft reached an altitude of 28,000 feet, a parachute opened. A bigger one opened at 10,000 feet, helping to slow down *Friendship 7*. John hit the switch for the landing bag. This time a green light came on. The capsule hit the water. Within minutes, a navy ship pulled along side the spacecraft, and John popped out. He had become the first American to orbit Earth, and the country had a new hero.

Off to Washington

Back on Earth, John stayed in the public eye for weeks. He spoke at the United Nations. He rode in parades. In New York City, an estimated 4 million people lined the streets to cheer John as he drove by. John also met President John F. Kennedy and visited Congress. He told the lawmakers about the details of his flight. As he finished his speech, John said, "As knowledge of the universe in which we live increases, God grant us the wisdom and guidance to use it wisely."

John traveled the country making public

appearances. He also worked on missions for the other Mercury astronauts. But John wasn't sure if he'd ever make another space flight. NASA was not making any promises. Into 1963, he still didn't know what he was going to do next.

On November 22, 1963, Americans were stunned as they learned that President Kennedy had been shot and killed by an assassin. John shared the nation's grief for the dead president. Since his historic flight, John had become friendly with Kennedy and his family. John did not always agree with Kennedy's policies, but the two men shared some important beliefs. Both thought space exploration was good for America. It could inspire people to do great things in all parts of life. And both John and the president believed the federal government should help people in need. Now, Kennedy's death helped give John a new direction.

"Annie," John said to his wife, "I think I'm going to leave NASA."

"Are you sure? N-n-no more flying?"

"I want to serve my country in other ways."

"S-such as?"

"How does 'Senator Glenn' sound to you?"

"P-politics?" Annie said. "You want to be a s-senator? From Ohio?"

"Yup. Let's go back home. I think I've done all I can do in the space business."

On January 17, 1964, John started his first political campaign. Some of John's friends from NASA helped him with his campaign. He didn't have much money, but John wanted to give the election his best shot. His race, however, ended before it really began. One morning, John had an accident in the bathroom. He slipped on a rug and hit his head on the bathtub. The blow knocked him out. He quickly regained his senses, but the fall damaged his head. He couldn't get out of bed for weeks.

"I can't run a campaign from a hospital bed," John said with disgust.

"I c-c-can go out for you," Annie offered. "We can still try."

John shook his head. "No, Annie, that's it. I'm

out of the race." He forced a laugh. "This is crazy."

"Wh-what?"

"I survived enemy fire and a mission in space, but I can't even make it out of my own bathroom."

On January 1, 1965, John officially retired from the marines. He entered the business world, working for Royal Crown, a large soft-drink company. He stayed active in politics by supporting other candidates. In 1968, Bobby Kennedy, President Kennedy's brother, ran for president. John worked for his campaign. In June, John was shocked to hear Bobby had been assassinated, just as his brother had been. At the funeral, John helped carry the coffin.

During these years, John kept the idea of serving in Washington. In 1970, he announced another try for the U.S. Senate. First he had to run against another Democrat, Howard Metzenbaum. The two politicians competed in an election called a primary. The winner of the primary would face a Republican opponent in November. This time John was healthy and he campaigned hard. Still, he lost the race to Metzenbaum, who then lost in November.

"I'm not giving up," John told Annie. "I'll run again. And this time, I'll win."

John got his chance in 1974. Once again, Metzenbaum was his opponent in the Democratic primary. John had less money than Metzenbaum did, but once again he worked hard. And John knew what to do when Metzenbaum made a big mistake.

"Look at this," Annie said, showing John a newspaper. Her stutter was now almost completely gone. In 1973, she had tried a new therapy that helped her tremendously.

"I can't believe what Metzenbaum said about you."

John examined the paper. "I've never had a job?" John exploded. "He said I've never had a job!"

"What are you going to do?" Annie asked

"We have that big debate in Cleveland coming up. I'll have a few words for Mr. Metzenbaum then."

At the debate, the two men explained what they would do as a senator. John waited till the end of the evening to respond to Metzenbaum's charge.

"Howard, how could you ever say I've never had a job? I proudly served in the Marines for twenty-three years. I flew more than one hundred combat missions in two wars. Did you ever serve in the military, Howard?"

Metzenbaum was silent. He had not served.

"Up in space, my life was on the line. That was a job, too, Howard. You should be on your knees thanking God that there are people who have had the kinds of jobs I've done. They love their country and are dedicated to their duty. That love and dedication are more important than life itself. Howard, I have held a job."

The crowd of six hundred people stood and clapped. National papers reported John's stirring speech. The primary came just a few days later, and John won by one hundred thousand votes. A few months later, John easily beat his Republican opponent. He was finally going to the U.S. Senate.

In the Senate, John was assigned to the Foreign Relations Committee. He also served on the Government Operations Committee.

"That's an important one," John told Annie. "We can look into activity of the federal government. We make sure they're not wasting money or doing anything illegal. If there's something wrong, we can fix it."

"You always want to make things better, hmm?" Annie said.

"Nothing wrong with trying."

For the next six years, John worked hard in Washington. He took an interest in military issues and relations with the Soviet Union. The Cold War was still underway, and John wanted to try to reduce the number of weapons each side had. In 1980, the voters of Ohio reelected him to the Senate. Ronald Reagan, a Republican, was elected president that year. John did not always like Reagan's policies.

"We have a million more people out of work," John said to Annie. "And Reagan wants to cut back on federal money for the poor. Those people didn't ask to lose their jobs."

"He wants a smaller government, right?" Annie asked.

"So he says."

"What do you think?"

"I don't want the government interfering in people's lives," John said. "But it does have a role to play. Sometimes the government has to help people who can't help themselves. Look at the Depression—the government's programs helped a lot of our friends and their families in New Concord."

Annie nodded. "What are you going to do?"

"I can't take much more of Reagan and his policies. They're cruel medicine for the poor." John took his wife's shoulders. "Annie, what would you think if I ran for president of the United States?"

Anne smiled. "I think you'd make a great president."

On April 21, 1983, John went to New Concord to announce that he was running for president. He would be competing against other Democrats in primaries across the country. The winner of the most primaries would face Reagan in November 1984. John's strongest opponent was Walter Mondale. He had served as vice president from 1977 to 1981 under President Jimmy Carter. Mondale was considered the likely winner for the Democrats. But John planned to campaign hard.

The New Concord High School band played at John's speech. The school was now named for Glenn. So was a street in his hometown. John told the crowd, "I want to talk about all the values that made me what I am. I believe in excellence, honesty, fairness, and compassion. I say it's time America was on the march to better things. My slogan is, 'Believe in the Future Again.'"

John began to travel across the country seeking support. Annie traveled with him. Lyn, who was now married, sometimes went with her father, too. John repeated his message of hope over and over. He also attacked Reagan's policies. By January 1984, John had campaign offices in forty-three states. But running a presidential campaign was not easy. "I don't know if we can make it," he said to Annie. "We lost pretty badly in Iowa."

"Fifth place is not so good," Annie agreed. "Maybe . . . maybe you should quit now."

John winced. "I hate that word—'quit.' There's got to be a way to hold on. We can borrow some more money. We might do better on Super Tuesday. What do you think?"

"Super Tuesday" was on March 13. Democratic voters in a number of states would go to the polls. If John won some of the primaries on that day, he would still have a chance.

"You're right," Annie said. "Why not try it?"

"Right," John said, sounding more confident. "After all, I've done riskier things in my life."

The night of Super Tuesday, John, Annie, and the campaign staff gathered at John's office.

"It doesn't look good," one aide said. "You're not even close in any of the states."

"This is it," John said. "I have to get out."

Three days later, John announced that he was leaving the race for president. Still, his political career wasn't over. He still had his senate seat. "Although my campaign for the presidency will end," John said, "my campaign for a better America will continue."

The Last Flight

"I want to go back into space."

Annie put down her newspaper and looked up at John.

"I think there's something wrong with my ears," Annie said. "I thought you just said something like, 'I want to go back into space.'"

"You know that's exactly what I said." John sat down next to his wife. "Annie, I've been thinking about this a lot."

It was December 1995. John was now seventy-four years old. A veteran senator (he served four consecutive terms), he was still interested in NASA and its activities. He had an idea how he could serve his country one more time.

"I've just read this book," John said. "It talks about the problems astronauts face in space. Physical changes. They're the same kind of health problems some people deal with when they get to be our age. Things like not sleeping well, weakening muscles. The only difference is, the astronauts' bodies recover when they come back to Earth."

"What does this have to do with you going into space?" Annie asked.

"Maybe if scientists study an older person in space, they can find a way to help the astronauts. Or to help ease the health problems of the elderly here on Earth."

"And you think you're the old man they should send into space to find this out."

"Why not?" John said. "I'm still in good shape. I know how NASA works. And, Annie, I want to fly above Earth one last time."

Annie shook her head. "John Glenn, I think you are going crazy. I don't like it, not at all. But I won't stop you. I just hope the government has enough sense to tell you no."

Since 1962, space exploration had gone far beyond John's flight in *Friendship 7.* Astronauts had floated in space and walked on the moon. Spacecraft had landed on Mars and sent back pictures of other planets. Astronauts had lived on space stations for months at a time. Now the United States was using space shuttles to conduct experiments in space. These craft could fly many missions and return to Earth by landing on runways, just as planes do.

Space travel, however, still had dangers. In 1986, Americans watched their TVs with horror during the liftoff of the shuttle *Challenger.* Barely a minute into its flight, the shuttle exploded, killing all seven astronauts onboard. As always, John didn't think about what could go wrong on his return to space. He thought about having the chance to serve his country, and the whole world, in a new way.

John spent two years convincing NASA it should send an elderly person into space. He argued he was the right astronaut for the mission. John also had to pass all the physical tests required for current astronauts. Finally, on January 16, 1998, NASA made an announcement. John Glenn was going to be the seventh crew member on the shuttle *Discovery* during an upcoming mission.

Life became very busy for NASA's newest—and oldest—astronaut. John flew back and forth between Washington and Houston, the flight center for the shuttle missions. He kept up with his work in the Senate as he prepared for the flight. Just as in the Mercury days, he had to study books and take training sessions. John also went through medical tests. Doctors took blood samples, measured his bones, and x-rayed his body. They would repeat these tests after the flight, to see if his body had changed while in space.

As the launch date neared, John's excitement grew. So did the country's. The news media paid a lot of attention to the mission. Millions of Americans had not been alive in 1962. Now they learned about John's earlier heroics. And he was becoming a hero all over again. At seventy-seven, John was about to become the oldest person ever to go into space. Other elderly Americans were proud of him. He was showing that old age did not stop people from having exciting and productive lives.

Once at an airport, an elderly couple stopped John.

"Senator Glenn," said the man, "you have changed my life."

"How's that?" John wondered.

"Ever since I was a boy, I wanted to climb mountains. But I grew up and got a job and never did. Then I got married and raised a family. Mountain climbing became a faded dream. Then I read about your flight."

"And?"

"Well, I thought if John Glenn can go back into space at seventy-seven, then I can climb a mountain. My wife and I are going to Africa to climb Mount Kilimanjaro!"

John shook the man's hand. "It's nice to know I've inspired you," he said.

"Not just me, Senator. Not just me."

On October 29, 1998, John and the other crew members on *Discovery* lifted off into space. After a few hours, Flight Commander Curt Brown sent a message to Earth. "Let the record show that John has a smile on his face and it goes from one ear to the other and we haven't been able to remove it yet."

For eight days, John performed experiments and lived in zero gravity. He ate food that came in small tubes. He slept in a sleeping bag attached to the shuttle. He brushed his teeth with special toothpaste.

"No foam or bubbles," John said, looking into a mirror.

He also sent e-mails to Annie. He wrote that everything was going well and he missed her. "And thank you once again," he typed, "for letting me go. This is truly a dream come true."

When *Discovery* landed, John had made 134 orbits of Earth. Back in 1962, he had made just three. The shuttle and its crew had traveled more than 3.6 million miles. Inside the craft, John sent a message to Houston. He echoed his words on his first trip into space. "One G," he said, "and I feel fine."

The flight was over, but John's work wasn't. He went through another round of medical tests.

"You're in fine shape, John," one of the doctors said. "There seems to be no reason why other elderly people can't go into space."

"That's what I thought all along," John said.

"And once we study these results, we may know more about the aging process here on Earth. Thanks, John."

John shook the doctor's hand. "Just trying to do what I can."

Soon after *Discovery*'s flight, John left the Senate. He wanted to spend more time with Annie, their children, and their grandchildren. He also wanted to teach. Ohio State University opened the John Glenn Institute, where students could study politics and public service.

John's entire life is about public service. He fought for his country in war. He risked his life to explore space. He went to Washington to help others. Through his actions, John Glenn offered an example that others could follow. He always tries his best, and usually he succeeds at what he wants to do. Even after his last space flight, John was eager to do more. He said, "I expect the future to bring new rewards and challenges." John Glenn has always shown he was ready for challenges.

Acknowledgments

Most of the information for this book came from John Glenn's 1999 autobiography, *John Glenn: A Memoir* (Bantam Doubleday Dell, 1999). Other useful sources included *Glenn: The Astronaut Who Would Be President,* by Frank Van Riper; *We Seven,* a collection of writings by the seven Mercury astronauts; a documentary on Glenn produced by the A & E cable network; and various newspaper and magazine articles.

Chronology

1918: John Herschel Glenn and Clara Sproat marry.

1921: John Herschel Glenn, Jr., is born on July 18, 1921, in Cambridge, Ohio.

1929: John takes his first plane ride.

1932: John and a group of friends form the Ohio Rangers, their own version of the Boy Scouts.

1935: John enters New Concord High School.

1937: John is elected president of his junior class.

1939: John enters Muskingum College.

1941: John earns his pilot license; America enters World War II.

1942: John enlists in the U.S. Navy and begins training as a military pilot. He later joins the U.S. Marines.

1943: John weds his childhood sweetheart, Annie Castor.

1944: Serving in the Marshall Islands, John makes his first combat flight.

1945: World War II ends; John chooses to remain in the marines for his career and become a test pilot; son John David Glenn is born on December 13.

1946: John briefly serves in China, flying patrol missions.

1947: Daughter Carolyn Ann (Lyn) Glenn is born on March 15.

1950: The Korean War begins.

1953: John flies fighter jets in Korea and shoots down

three Soviet MiG jets.

1957: John sets a new record for the fastest flight across the United States; the Soviet Union launches the first satellite into orbit.

1959: John is one of seven men chosen to be America's first astronauts.

1961: Soviet cosmonaut (astronaut) Yuri Gagarin is the first person to orbit Earth.

1962: John is the first American to orbit Earth.

1963: President John F. Kennedy is assassinated.

1964: John enters his first campaign for the U.S. Senate but soon pulls out of the race.

1965: John leaves the marines and enters business.

1969: The United States puts the first astronauts on the moon.

1970: John again runs for the U.S. Senate.

1974: John is elected a U.S. senator from Ohio.

1980: John wins reelection to the Senate.

1983: John announces his decision to run for the U.S. presidency.

1984: John drops out of the race for president.

1986: John wins reelection to the Senate.

1998: John flies on the shuttle *Discovery*, becoming the oldest person ever in space.